Bear took off with the ball in his jowls, sending both Wes and Jack scrambling after him from opposite directions, colliding in a jumble of bare calves and black fur and laughter.

A moment later Wes sat up, grinning like a goon, the ball held aloft…but only until Jack snatched it from him a moment later.

Blythe laughed, the sound apparently reaching Wes on the same breeze that toyed with her already crazed hair, soothing skin she hadn't realized was heated. Which heated more when a panting, grinning, messy-haired Wes glanced over. Oh, my.

"Come join us," he yelled, raking a hand through that hair. Flashing those damn dimples. "You can be on the dog's team."

I can't, she wanted to say. Needed to say.

I can't, because I have to get back home, to my safe, solitary little life, the one where there's no dimpled, sexy, stalwart man tugging at my heart and his young, needy son tugging even harder.

Dear Reader,

Although easygoing Blythe Broussard will already be familiar to readers of my first two Summer Sisters books (*The Doctor's Do-Over* and *A Gift for All Seasons*), just like them I knew who she was only through her cousins' eyes. Not until I started writing her story did she finally cough up her secrets…and the pain and insecurities brought about by those secrets. Thus Blythe and I—and Wes Phillips, the last man Blythe has any business falling in love with—began quite the journey of discovery, a journey that eventually frees this loving, generous character from an emotional bondage that shackled her for far too long…just as it does far too many people in the real world.

So to all my readers who may be struggling with a similar situation, or know someone who is, I dedicate this story, hoping it might serve as an inspiration—or a kick in the pants! Because we don't conquer our fears by hiding from them, but by facing them down, by learning from them and moving forward. We all make mistakes, and we all deserve forgiveness…starting with forgiving ourselves.

Blessings,

Karen Templeton

THE MARRIAGE CAMPAIGN

KAREN TEMPLETON

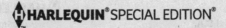
HARLEQUIN® SPECIAL EDITION®

Recycling programs
for this product may
not exist in your area.

ISBN-13: 978-0-373-65724-7

THE MARRIAGE CAMPAIGN

Copyright © 2013 by Karen Templeton-Berger

Printed in U.S.A.

www.Harlequin.com

Books by Karen Templeton

Harlequin Special Edition

§*Husband Under Construction* #2120
‡*Fortune's Cinderella* #2161
‡‡*The Doctor's Do-Over* #2211
‡‡*A Gift for All Seasons* #2223
‡‡*The Marriage Campaign* #2242

Silhouette Special Edition

**Baby Steps #1798
***The Prodigal Valentine* #1808
***Pride and Pregnancy* #1821
††*Dear Santa* #1864
††*Yours, Mine... or Ours?* #1876
††*Baby, I'm Yours* #1893
§*A Mother's Wish* #1916
§*Reining in the Rancher* #1948
††*From Friends to Forever* #1988
§*A Marriage-Minded Man* #1994
§*Welcome Home, Cowboy* #2054
§*Adding Up to Marriage* #2073

Harlequin Romantic Suspense

†*Plain-Jane Princess* #1096
†*Honky-Tonk Cinderella* #1120
What a Man's Gotta Do #1195
Saving Dr. Ryan #1207
Fathers and Other Strangers #1244
Staking His Claim #1267
♦*Everybody's Hero* #1328
♦*Swept Away* #1357
♦*A Husband's Watch* #1407

Yours Truly

*Wedding Daze
*Wedding Belle
**Wedding? Impossible!*

**Babies, Inc.
†How to Marry a Monarch
*Weddings, Inc.
♦The Men of Mayes County
††Guys and Daughters
§Wed in the West
‡The Fortunes of Texas:
    Whirlwind Romance
‡‡Summer Sisters

Other titles by this author
available in ebook format.

KAREN TEMPLETON

Since 1998, two-time RITA® Award winner and Walden-books bestselling author Karen Templeton has written more than thirty novels for Harlequin Books. A transplanted Easterner, she now lives in New Mexico with two hideously spoiled cats and whichever of her five sons happens to be in residence.

Chapter One

It wasn't that Blythe Broussard hated Valentine's Day as much as she had no real use for it. Like camping gear. Or a garlic press. Not that she was above glomming half-price chocolate the day after—if she happened to be out and there it was, languishing. Because if bargain chocolate was involved, what did she care what kind of box it came in?

Not that there hadn't been a time when she'd wake up on Valentine's Day, hope blooming in her heart that she'd maybe at least get a *card* from a boy in her class. However, those memories were as relegated to the past as the few cards she'd received, from the few boys not intimated by a girl who, by the fourth grade, towered over them— an imbalance Mother Nature hadn't rectified until well into high school.

At which point Blythe latched on to the first boy whose eyes met hers without getting a crick in his neck. And he, her. With far more enthusiasm than expertise. Or staying power. Unfortunately, by the time Blythe realized her deflowering was going to be memorable, all right, but for all the wrong reasons, it was too late to ask for her virginity back.

And, naturally, said inauspicious event happened on Valentine's Day. Fourteen years ago to the day, Blythe thought morosely, slumped in the faded blue velvet couch in the wannabe chichi bridal shoppe—yes, with the extra *p* and *e*—while her cousins Mel and April tried on bridal gowns in adjoining dressing rooms, for their double wedding four months hence. For which Blythe, God help her, had not only agreed to be their maid of honor, but to coordinate the event. Because decorating people's houses somehow qualified her to be a wedding planner.

But as children, when they'd spent their summers together at their grandmother's house in nearby St. Mary's Cove on Maryland's Eastern Shore, the three had been like sisters. Despite drifting apart as teens, when they'd reunited some six months before to settle their late grandmother's estate, it was as though the intervening decade had never happened. So Blythe would do anything for them.

Even plan their weddings.

Beside her, Mel's ten-year-old daughter, Quinn, squealed, then bounced off the love seat and over to the window, her bright red curls glimmering in the pearly light.

"Look, Blythe! It's finally snowing!"

Sure enough, fat, lazy snowflakes floated from a flannelled sky, already clinging, Blythe realized when she joined Quinn, to the strip mall's sidewalk. She frowned, not looking forward to driving across icy bay bridges to get back to her house in Alexandria, on the outskirts of Washington.

"So it is," Blythe said, checking her cell phone for the

time. Two hours, they'd already been here. Behind her, she heard April's musical giggle from the nearest dressing room. *Please, God,* she thought as she returned to her seat, *let this be The One...*

Quinn tromped back to join her, her momentary excitement about the snow yielding to the agony that was waiting for not one, but *two* brides to decide on their gowns. On a huge yawn, she collapsed against Blythe's side. Smiling, Blythe wrapped one arm around her younger cousin's shoulders. "Remember, you *wanted* to come along."

"Because I thought it would be fun. Jeez, how long can it take to pick out a stupid white dress?"

Blythe chuckled, even though she totally empathized. "It's a process," she said, cramming memories of her own wedding back inside her jam-packed brain. Although she hadn't spent much longer picking her outfit—first white suit she saw, done—than she had her groom. Perhaps if she had, she'd still be married.

Or not. Although Giles hadn't been...untalented, she thought with a quick twist to her mouth. Unfortunately, "talent" by itself hadn't been a strong enough glue to keep them together. Which they both admitted, divvying out the blame for their marriage's demise three years ago as equitably as they had the Williams-Sonoma cookware and Pottery Barn lamps.

At least April and Mel, now running their grandmother's inn, had both picked good men, men who were crazy about them, but not crazy. And both cousins seemed so confident in their choices, their love bubbling from some perpetually flowing spring Blythe could never quite seem to find—

"Ohmigosh, Mom!" Quinn popped up straight when her radiant mother appeared in a draped, corseted satin gown. "You look *amazing!*"

Kid did not exaggerate. Not only did the gown hug Mel's

generous curves in all the right places, but it was…Mel. Simple but not plain, elegant but sexy as hell. Exactly like the brunette wearing it, her gray-green eyes glittering underneath dark brown bangs.

"Oh, God, Mel…" While the thought of getting married again made Blythe break out in hives, she was truly happy for her cousin. After ten years of single motherhood, the woman deserved the something wonderful that was Dr. Ryder Caldwell, whom Mel had loved even as a little girl. "You look so damn good in that dress I could choke. And don't you dare repeat that," she said to Quinn, who rolled her eyes before rushing to her mother and hugging her.

A moment later their youngest cousin, April, swished out from the dressing room in a beaded, strapless, tulle confection that oddly didn't swallow the gingery blonde's petite figure.

"April!" Mel said, planting her hands on her hips when April climbed up beside her on the platform. "Holy cannoli."

"You got that right," April said, her huge grin the only thing brighter than the blingified bodice, flashing like mad underneath the salon's lights. Of course the alterations department would have to lop a good foot off the front of April's hem and do some creative molding around Mel's ample boobage but, other than that, the dresses were bang on. And, as different as they were, complemented rather than competed with each other.

"Well, come on—jack us up!" April said, waggling her hands at the two black-outfitted, smugly grinning consultants standing off to the side. A minute later, April sported a beaded, elbow-length veil that made her look like a fricking Madonna, while Mel opted for a clutch of silk camellias over her left ear. And it was all amazing and wonderful and too perfect for words.

As opposed to the weather, which, Blythe was horrified to note, was not.

Because by the time both brides were back in their regular clothes, the fluffy, lazy flakes had given way to a blizzard. A blizzard not even April's hotsy-totsy Lexus, in which they'd all trooped up from St. Mary's, was going to like a whole lot.

So much for getting back to D.C. Or anywhere, for that matter, a thought that made Blythe's head hurt.

Or her cousins any too happy, either, apparently. The two cousins with Big Plans for the evening, what with it being Valentine's Day and all.

"Can you drive in this?" Mel asked April as they pushed through the glass doors into the snow scene from *The Nutcracker.* But without the magic factor. Or the glorious music.

"I grew up in Richmond, what do you think?" April sighed out, then looked from Blythe to Mel. "I'm good with either of you driving, though—"

"No way," Mel said, draping a protective arm around her daughter before spearing Blythe with her gaze. "And don't even think about it. The way you drive in ideal conditions is scary enough."

"Hey—!"

"And the pair of you," April put in, shivering inside her jacket as she put her phone to her ear, "can hush up right now. There's a Howard Johnson's just across the street. And that big supermarket over there." Both of which were barely visible through the wall of snow. "So if we're stranded, at least they won't find us dead of starvation in the car."

Always the optimist, that April. "What about your guests?" Blythe asked.

"In February? Not to worry, we don't have any bookings for the next two weeks—" She held up one finger as whoever she'd called answered. "Hey, sugar," she said, in all likelihood to her fiancé Patrick. "It's snowing real bad here, it looks like we're stuck...."

This in stereo with Mel's having virtually the same conversation on Blythe's other side with *her* honey. Blythe, of course, had no one to call, no one to worry about her. Or disappoint that she wouldn't make it home tonight. No one who'd even know or care that she was marooned in some lame strip mall in a town so tiny it didn't even show up on MapQuest unless you hit the magnify dealiebobber five times. Most of the time, she found it liberating, even exhilarating, not having to answer to anybody about her comings and goings. Tonight, though...

Probably something to do with the drop in the barometric pressure.

"Okay, I'm gonna go snag a couple of rooms," April said, all sparkly-eyed and whatnot. God bless her. "So why don't y'all go get some food? I'll make sure there's a fridge in one of the rooms..."

And off she went, trudging through the storm like the intrepid little pioneer woman she was clearly channeling. Nobody could accuse any of them of being wimps, that was for sure, Blythe thought as she scurried to catch up to Mel and Quinn, laughing like a pair of goons as they slipped and slid across the parking lot.

"Ohmigosh," Quinn yelped as they got closer to the store, swarmed with people clearly convinced this was Armageddon. "Look...it's Jack and his dad!"

Jack, being Quinn's good buddy Jack Phillips, who lived a few houses down from the inn, and Jack's *dad* being Blythe's worst nightmare.

Or fantasy, depending on where her dreams decided to take her on any given night.

As if she needed this day, or her headache, to get any worse.

Oh, yes, Blythe was well acquainted with Wes Phillips, he of the dimpled, dashing politician's grin that had, in all likelihood, gone a long way toward garnering the freshman congressman sixty-two percent of his district's vote in the last election—despite Wes's being that oddest of odd ducks, an independent candidate. Along with, Blythe had to reluctantly admit, policies that made him as easy on the nerves as he was on the eyes. Because the dimples came as part of a package that included honest, direct hazel eyes—complete with sexy crinkles, natch—and a jawline that would make Michelangelo weep. Also, he was tall. As in, tall enough that she could be standing in front of him in four-inch-heels—like, say, now—and those damn bedroom eyes were still level with hers.

But.

Since this was one of those never-gonna-happen things, for many, *many* reasons, Wes Phillips could darn well keep his eyes and his jaw and his dimples to himself, thank you, and Blythe would content herself with the occasional, random, toe-curling dream, and all would be well.

"Ladies! What on earth are you all doing out in this nasty weather?"

"Um…bridal gown shopping," Mel said in a might-as-well-come-right-out-with-it voice. Sure enough, Wes's smile faltered. Not a lot, but enough if you knew what you were looking at. In this case, what Mel's upcoming wedding probably meant to a man who'd lost his wife in the same car crash two years before that had also killed Ryder's fiancée Deanna. While Mel's return to St. Mary's had obviously been instrumental in binding Ryder's wounds, Wes was clearly still grieving.

Reason Number One why Blythe had to ignore the dimples.

And Reason Number Two would be his son, who, even while talking to Quinn, shot a hurt-littered glance at her mother. As often as Blythe had hauled Quinn and Jack around over the past few months, she'd had plenty of opportunities to observe, and listen to, eleven-year-old Jack. Caught in that horrible limbo between childhood and adolescence, the boy bore all the earmarks of a good kid ready to erupt—earmarks Blythe knew all too well. Earmarks she wished she knew how to alert his father to without sounding like a buttinski. Or, worse, like she was looking for a way to make herself, you know. Available.

Because—and this would be Reason Number Three, aka the Biggee—making herself available had only ever led to heartbreak and confusion and wondering why she'd even bothered.

However, the good news was that she'd finally caught on, that she was a much saner, nicer person alone than when she was in a relationship. So, hallelujah, she'd never have to fight for the bedcovers again—

"And what brings you out?" Mel said to Wes, and the smile ratcheted up again.

"The usual," he said, hunkering down farther into his olive-green down parka. "Meeting with constituents, getting an earful. Trying to reassure while not making promises I know I can't keep."

Oh, and there was the issue of Wes being a politician. Almost immaterial on top of everything else, but definitely a contributing factor to Blythe's ignoring how he was looking at her right now. Because she knew all too well what life was like for politicians, having worked with plenty of clients in the trenches. Or close to those who were. Their work was their life, the hours often horrendously long when they were in Washington, their time at "home" still eaten up with travel and meetings and glad-handing the people who'd voted them into office. That is, if one was the conscientious sort, which, from everything she could tell, Wes was. For that, she had to give the man props—

Mel looked around. "No entourage?"

Wes chuckled. "Not today. Sometimes I just get in the car and drive, stopping where the mood strikes, see if anyone's up for chatting." Dimples flashed. "Someone usually is." His expression softening, he smiled for his son. "Gives Jack and me a chance to hang out. Catch up."

But it was that very conscientiousness that caused, she had no doubt, the look she'd seen all too often in his son's eyes—the son still smarting over his mother's loss. It sometimes made her want to smack Wes Phillips upside the head.

True, it was none of her business. Nor was the kid neglected—Wes's parents lived with Wes and Jack, and seemed to be the most doting grandparents ever. But still. It was obvious how much the kid needed, wanted, his dad. And how much he resented having to share him with the entire Eastern Shore. And, having endured similar crappage from her own parents while growing up, Blythe's heart broke for the boy.

Meaning there was no way she'd ever let his father anywhere near it.

Dimples be damned.

Happened every damn time he saw her, that kick to the gut that made Wes wonder if he was losing it. Because it was insane, the way Blythe Broussard got his juices flowing. Insane, and inexplicable, and highly inconvenient, what with his barely having time to figure out the *why* behind the insane, inexplicable attraction, let alone pursue it. Even if he wanted to, which he didn't. He didn't think.

But there she stood, holding his gaze hostage even from several feet away. Man, she looked at him like she wanted to do a feng shui number on his brain, her eyes huge, somehow accusing, a weird shade of deep blue in a pale, sharp-boned face. Her hair was almost as short as his and nearly a white-blond, her mouth a dark red few women could pull off and not look macabre.

She wasn't even pretty, not in a conventional sense. And so unlike Kym, who had been. Still. Juices. Flowing.

Like the flippin' Potomac.

He deliberately turned to Mel, as short and curvy as Blythe was tall and...not. "So are you headed back to St. Mary's?"

The brunette snorted. "In this?" She gestured toward the snow, now coming down as if intent on beating all previous records. "No way."

Wes liked Mel, was more grateful than he could say that her daughter, Quinn, and Jack had become close friends. Losing his mom and then, ipso facto, Wes as well, had been rough on the kid. And he was glad, he really was, that Ryder had been able to move on after Deanna's death. But then, he hadn't known her—loved her—for twenty years, as Wes had Kym.

"We decided to camp out at HoJo for the night," Mel said. "And you?"

"Now that you mention it...I'm not wild about driving in this, either. Hey, Jack!" He called over to the two kids, standing in the parking lot, trying to catch snowflakes on their tongues. "You okay with hanging out here tonight?"

The kid turned. "At the Food Lion?"

"No, goof—at the hotel over there." Then his eyes grazed Blythe's, and the punch to his chest knocked his breath sideways. Not that he'd doubted the attraction was largely sexual, but after all those months of feeling like he'd mainlined Lidocaine…holy hell.

Must be the weather. Or the buzz left over from the afternoon's schmoozings, reminding him of the reason he tossed his hat in the ring to begin with. That he'd left it there even after…

Wes jerked his gaze, and his thoughts, back to Mel. "If there's a room…?"

"I'll see if April can book a third room," she said, pulling out her phone as Blythe walked away, dodging a family coming out of the store, their three kids jumping around like snowsuited fleas. And he saw her smile, watching them, before their eyes met again and she flicked the smile off like a switch and turned away. Right. Because maybe all that gut-kicking and chest-punching had less to do with sex than it did aversion. On her part, that is.

Hey, it happened. He was a politician, after all, even if the term still didn't feel right, like a pair of new shoes he couldn't seem to break in. Plenty of people disliked him, simply because their vision didn't mesh with his. Just came with the territory. And God knew nothing to get his boxers in a bunch over, even if his time in office—not to mention his campaign manager and half his staff—would try to convince him he was too nice for his own good.

Well, tough, he thought, as Mel gave him a thumbs-up—about the room, he presumed, before ducking into the store with the kids—because while sacrifice also came with the territory, he wasn't about to slap his integrity on the altar. For anyone. Or anything. He'd thrown his hat in the ring for his own reasons, reasons many might consider idealistic, even naive. But at the end of the day none of it meant diddly if he lost his self-respect. Not to mention his son's.

"You're not going in with them?" he called to Blythe.

She glanced over, then shrugged. "Nah, I'm good with whatever Mel gets."

Wes nodded, feeling oddly out of his depth. Closing arguments, no problem. Ditto giving speeches, or discussing issues with constituents. Although he wasn't an attention seeker for its own sake, neither was he an introvert. Words, ideas, usually came easily to him, and one of his "gifts" was his ability to work a crowd. And yet, he hadn't felt this tongue-tied around a woman since those agonizing months in the ninth grade working up to asking Kym out.

Not that this was anything like that, of course.

He closed the space between them, wondering what she was looking at so hard out in the parking lot. Boldly, Wes regarded her profile, the harsh, storefront lighting emphasizing the almost grim set to her mouth.

"Flurries, the weatherman said," she said.

Wes faced the lot, his hands in his pockets. "Ridiculous, isn't it?"

"Do they ever get it right?"

"Not a whole lot, no." He cleared his throat. "So did your cousins find their dresses?"

"What? Oh. Yes. They did."

"Weddings," he said, shaking his head, remembering.

After a long pause, she said, "Was yours large?"

He shoved out a breath through his nose. "Yeah." He laughed. "I barely remember it, though."

"Too drunk?"

Surprised at the tease—if that's what it was—he laughed. "No. Too scared. Not that I didn't want it—I would've married Kym at eighteen, if I could have—but when the day came, I panicked. You know—what am I doing? What if it doesn't work out? That sort of thing. Then she started down the aisle, and all I saw was her smile…" He shook his head. "And for the rest of the night

I blotted out everything *but* that smile. Only thing that got me through."

A long pause preceded, "I'm sorry. Not about your wedding, about—"

"I know what you meant. Thanks."

Blythe nodded, wrapping her arms around herself. "So. Guess we're all stuck with each other tonight."

"I wouldn't worry too hard about it," Wes said, ridiculously irked. "After all, we probably won't even be on the same floor. So we wouldn't, you know, have to see each other."

Beside him, he heard her mighty sigh. "So much for hoping that didn't sound as bitchy as it did in my head—"

Mel and the children burst out of the store, all carting bulging plastic bags. "Let's hear it for self-checkout lanes!" Mel said, then started across the lot, her yakking charges in tow.

"We should probably follow," Wes said, moving to take Blythe's elbow; not surprisingly, she avoided him. Whatever. Still hugging herself, she cautiously stepped into the rapidly accumulating slush, completely at the mercy of her high-heeled boots. Ahead of them, Mel—in far more sensible flats—was deliberately skidding in the snow as much as the kids. Laughing as much, too.

No wonder Blythe's cousin been able to help Ryder move past his grief—even if they hadn't already been childhood friends, Mel was exactly what Ryder had needed. With a pang, Wes realized he was envious, that Ryder was getting a second chance at something Wes doubted he ever would. Because despite everyone—his parents, his campaign manager, even his dentist, for God's sake—pushing him to remarry, there'd never be anybody like Kym, ever.

The screech, not to mention the dramatic flailing, made

him jerk his head around, then down, to see Blythe on her butt in the snow, swearing like a sergeant.

Grinning, he held out his hand. And prayed the woman wouldn't bite it off.

Chapter Two

Her head now pounding, Blythe stared at Wes's outstretched hand, momentarily considering refusing to let him help her up. Except grace had never been her strong suit in the best of circumstances; in four inches of slippery slop she'd probably look like a drunken giraffe.

"You okay?" Wes said, as he hauled her to her feet.

"Yeah, yeah, I'm fine," she grumbled, swatting her backside to dislodge the worst of the snow clumps. "Although my dignity will never live this down."

"Hey. I haven't seen hide nor hair of my dignity in years. I've learned to live without it."

Still swatting, Blythe slid her gaze to his, clearly amused behind the curtain of falling snow, and damn if her insides didn't do a tiny *ba-dump*. Then she sighed. "Thanks."

"Anytime." He lifted his elbow. And one eyebrow. Reluctantly—oh so reluctantly—she accepted. Despite the very likely possibility she'd go down again and take him with her. And, of course, the instant the thought zipped through, she slipped again. Man didn't even falter. In fact, he easily gripped her waist, effectively bonding her to his ribs. Steady as a rock, this one.

"So I'm guessing you don't hate me *that* much," he said.

Not to mention perceptive.

She wobbled again. And swore again. And, yes, Wes chuckled again. As he caught her.

"Swear to God," she gritted out, her head now feeling like the Riverdance people were practicing inside it, "I am not doing this on purpose."

"Didn't think you were. Since not even you could order this particular confluence of events." When she frowned up at him, he shrugged. And gave off a very nice man-scent that might have rendered a lesser woman addle-brained. "The snow. Those boots. My being here to keep you from breaking your neck."

"Or my ass," she muttered, and he grinned.

"That, too." As they came to a less snowy spot, he relaxed his hold. "*Are* you okay?"

Truth be told, her bum was smarting a bit. Not a whole lot of padding back there. Or anywhere else. At least that diverted her attention from her head. Sort of. "I'll live," she said as they reached the hotel's portico-covered driveway, where she wriggled out of his grasp. "I don't dislike you, Wes. Really. I just... I'm just tired and hungry and have a wicked headache. That's all."

The glass doors parted at their approach, but he touched her arm, holding her back. The dimples had taken a hike, praise be. But those eyes...

Oh, dear Lord, as April would say.

Ever since her divorce, Blythe had eschewed messing around. By choice. A choice she'd found, to both her surprise and immense relief, to be incredibly freeing to a woman who'd always thought of her libido as a pet to be cosseted and indulged. Within reason, anyway. But she'd come far closer than she'd realized to being a slave to that pet, resulting in some extremely poor choices along the way. So the "cleansing" period had finally allowed Blythe to begin to see who she really was, what she really needed.

And Wes Phillips's intense green gaze was *not* on that list.

"I'm sorry your head hurts—" he said gently.

Or his mouth.

"—but something tells me that look on your face is about more than your aching head. Unless I'm the one making your head hurt?"

Now that you mention it...

Even though her skull wasn't happy about it, Blythe laughed, ignoring the *ping-ping-ping* of neglected hormones perking up assorted places that hadn't been perky in quite a while.

"Only partly," she said, and he crossed his arms.

"Partly? Oh. Meaning you don't like my policies, I take it."

Blythe blew out a breath. "This isn't my district. I have no idea what your policies are." *Liar, liar...* "And I really don't feel up to talking, if you don't mind. At least not until I get some food in my stomach."

"Of course, I… Never mind. Come on."

Wes let her go through the automatic doors ahead of him, and the dry, warm air in the lobby enveloped her like a grandmother's hug—not *her* grandmother, but somebody's—as she joined Mel, April and the kids, clustered in front of the registration desk. Which was littered with every Valentine's tchotchke ever invented. Great.

"See you later?" Wes said shortly afterward, key card in hand. "In the restaurant?" When she frowned, that eyebrow lifted again. As well as the corners of that mouth. "You said you needed to eat?"

Blythe's eyes cut to the others, who were too busy yakking among themselves to witness the little exchange, thank God. "Depends on what Mel got at the store," she said. "Truthfully, all I want is to stretch out in a dark, quiet room until this blasted headache goes away."

His eyes twinkled. "Quiet? With that group?"

"If the gods are kind, they'll all congregate in the other room and leave me in peace."

"Well, if you change your mind—"

"Not likely," Blythe said as an infant's wail pierced her cousins' chatter, and Wes gave her something like a little bow.

"Have a good night, then," he and his dimples said. Then he ushered his son away, her gaze trailing after them like a confused, dumb puppy.

The puppy hauled back by the scruff of its neck, Blythe was about to break up the jabberfest when she noticed the bedraggled young father clutching the counter in front of the frowning clerk madly clicking her computer keys. Beside him, two young children clung like possums to his even more bedraggled wife, who was jiggling a wailing infant in her arms. Poor things.

"You guys ready to go up to the rooms?" Blythe said. "Don't know about you, but I'm about to crash."

"We figured we may as well hit the restaurant first," Mel said. "Since it's not as if we have luggage or anything."

"But…" Blythe frowned at the grocery bags, still in Mel's hands. "Didn't you buy food?"

"Munchies, mainly. Although there is a rotisserie chicken in there—"

"Close enough," Blythe said, grabbing the bags. "Give me a card, I'll see you guys later—"

"I'm so sorry," the clerk said to the little family, her words carrying across the lobby like she was wearing a mike, "but we just booked our last available rooms…"

April and Mel exchanged a blink-and-you'd-miss-it glance—which Blythe didn't—before April marched back to the clerk. "Give 'em one of our rooms. We gals can all bunk together. Right?"

So close. And yet, so far, Blythe thought, even as her hurting head threw a hissy fit. Then she looked again at the woman and her kids, and her heart kicked her throbbing head to the curb.

"Of course!" she said brightly. "Not like we all haven't shared a room before." If many, many years ago.

"Are you sure?" the wife said, shifting the bawling babe in her arms and managing to look miserable and grateful at the same time. "We wouldn't want to put you out."

"You're not. At all." Blythe smiled. "I swear."

Tears in her eyes, the young mother shifted the baby to hug all three of them in turn, and her cousins trooped to the restaurant and Blythe up to their room, where, for the next hour, she consoled herself with rotisserie chicken, potato salad and the eye-roll-worthy shenanigans of a bunch of surgically enhanced TV housewives whose lives were far more drama-ridden than hers.

Now, in any case. And considering what she'd gone through to get to this point, her hormones could just go hang themselves.

The next morning, Blythe wrenched open her eyes to total darkness, save for the pale gray chink in the closed draperies. As the others slept, she cautiously eased out of bed, cracking open the drapes enough to see the snow already melting, even in the weak winter sun. Hallelujah.

Then she caught her reflection in the mirror over the

dresser and grimaced. Fortunately her sweater and jeans were wear-again-worthy, even if she had to fend off the ickies of not being able to change her undies before facing the public again. But her hair…eesh. She could, however, wash up and brush her teeth—bless her hide, Mel had bought them all toothbrushes and a few essential toiletries—even if the only makeup she had in her purse was lipgloss.

Meaning, even cleaned up and redressed she looked like a vampire who hadn't had a good feed in a while. Or access to any decent hair care products, she mused as she doused her head with water from the spigot, then yanked a comb through her cropped hair until it looked…not horrible. With any luck, though—she clicked the door shut behind her and headed down the carpeted hall—she'd be the first one in the restaurant, and nobody would see her. Because the way her stomach was growling, Pringles and grapes weren't going to cut it. Especially when the elevator doors opened on the ground floor, and the scents of bacon and coffee and pancakes hauled her toward the restaurant's entrance like those little aliens did to Richard Dreyfuss in *Close Encounters.*

Blythe stood inside, breathing deeply for a moment until the hostess told her to sit anywhere she liked, and she rounded a huge potted plant to see that Wes and Jack had apparently beaten her by several minutes. Well, hell. She froze, watching, as the boy chattered away, his father leaning over his plate as he ate—bacon and eggs, Blythe saw—clearly intent on whatever Jack was saying. Occasionally, Wes would chuckle, pushing at those dimples, and the adoring expression on his son's face twisted Blythe inside out.

Then some woman barged in on the scene, interrupting Jack in the middle of a sentence to introduce herself to his father, and Blythe watched the kid's face collapse. True, apology flickered across Wes's features as he glanced at his son before standing to graciously acknowledge the woman, briefly introduce her to Jack, then listen as intently to her as he had a moment earlier to his child. Also true was the conflict evident in Wes's body language, that despite his graciousness he wasn't happy about having his private time with his son interrupted. But far worse, from her perspective, was the hurt and annoyance bowing Jack's slender shoulders as he frowned at his pancakes, shredding rather than eating them.

"Really, sit anywhere at all," the hostess said as she breezed past, and Blythe realized with a rush of heat to her face that she'd been staring.

"Right," she said, watching Wes hand the woman a card, along with a warm smile and a firm handshake before sending her on her way—

"Blythe!" Jack boomed. "Over here!"

So much for slipping into a booth out of their sight. But the way the child's face lit up...how could she say no? Although naturally they were sitting right next to a window, through which streamed that particularly bright, revealing, après-snowfall light.

Then again, maybe her vampire aura would scare away other potential intruders so Jack and Wes could finish their breakfast in peace.

Gamely, Blythe trekked over, clutching her purse to her empty middle. Once again seated and buttering a piece of toast, Wes looked up, tried—unsuccessfully—not to start, then smiled. He, of course, looked fabulous, in that sexy, beard-hazed way of a gorgeous man right out of bed. So unfair.

"Hey, there," he said, all gruff-voiced and such. "Join us?"

"I don't want to interrupt." When the merest suggestion

of a frown marred that handsome brow, she added, "You seemed…involved."

"She was a constituent," Wes said. "You're a friend. So sit," he said, waving his toast toward the other side of the booth as Blythe thought, *Friend? Really?* Then he smiled, the picture of solicitude. "How's your head?"

She sat beside Jack, who'd skootched over and was now grinning at her around an enormous bite of his pancakes, his too-long hair like corn silk in the silvery light. "Okay, actually."

Actually, she hadn't even noticed. The others, as worn out as Blythe from the events of the day, had all conked out fairly early, and Blythe had slept like a freaking rock. But Wes was frowning at her like she was trying to keep her game face on after being given a month to live.

"You sure?"

The waitress came, filled her coffee cup, handed her a menu. Blythe nearly smacked the poor kid with it in her eagerness to get coffee to her lips. Once she'd downed sufficient caffeine to hopefully put some color in her cheeks, she let her gaze flick to Wes. Which *definitely* put color in her cheeks. "Yes, I'm sure. I'm a little washed out without makeup. But thanks for asking."

She waved the waitress back over, ordered a breakfast worthy of a lumberjack, then turned aside to grin at Jack, exercising every ounce of willpower she possessed not to take her coffee spoon to his pancakes. Almost as much willpower as it was taking not to make goo-goo eyes at his father. Old habits dying hard and all that. She bumped shoulders with Jack. "Those look pretty good."

"They're okay. Want a bite?"

"No, you go ahead," she said, resting her chin in her hand. "I'll wait for my own food."

"Quinn awake yet?"

"She wasn't when I left, but she could be now." A light-bulb blinked on. "You want me to call her?" *And tell them to get their booties down here before I lose what little sanity I have left?*

"Oh, don't do that," Wes said with a pointed look at his son. "You can see Quinn later. At home." Then to Blythe, obligating her to look at him. "State Trooper was here earlier, said the roads are clear. We can leave any time."

"Thank goodness for that. I need to get back to D.C. to work on a presentation for tomorrow morning."

"Although the trooper did say it was a good thing we didn't try driving last night. Visibility was horrendous. And road conditions…" He shook his head. "Accidents all over the place."

"No one was hurt, I hope."

"No. But not for lack of trying."

Out of the corner of her eye, Blythe saw the young family file in, looking a lot more mellow than they had the night before. And right behind them, her cousins, none of whom looked like something the cat had dragged in. Mel had this whole mussed-bangs thing going on, and April was pink and pretty as usual with her peachy blond hair pulled back in a headband. And Quinn was ten, so there you were.

And before Blythe realized what was happening—or could have done anything about it—Jack asked if he could go sit with the others, and Wes said, "Sure," right as the waitress brought her food.

Well, hell.

Catching the momentary *Oh, crap* look in Blythe's eyes when Jack left, Wes was half tempted to let her off the hook, tell her to go join her cousins. Except fascination trumped logic, apparently, as he found himself unwilling to forgo more one-on-one time with her. Especially since he'd been mulling over something for a while now, anyway. So maybe this was fate tossing opportunity into his lap.

For the next few seconds, however, Wes contented himself with watching Blythe tuck into her huge breakfast, her pale lashes and brows gleaming in the harsh white light. Her skin was luminous, flawless, her prickly attitude so much at odds with what he now saw as her almost ethereal beauty—one she habitually obliterated with more makeup than she needed, in his opinion. A mask, he suspected, in more ways than one.

But there was an honesty and forthrightness to the prickliness he found refreshing. Nor did he miss her easy relationship with Jack—witnessing their short exchange earlier had made warmth curl inside his chest. It was also a nice change to be around someone who didn't want anything from him. Or so Wes assumed. He lifted his coffee cup to his lips, watching Blythe attack her breakfast.

"You're really going to eat all that?"

"I really am," she said, dumping an ocean's worth of syrup over her pancakes before forking in a huge bite. "As you may have noticed, I'm not exactly petite. Yogurt and juice is not going to cut it."

And maybe food was the antidote to the prickliness. Feeling a tug at his mouth, he said, "I have a favor to ask you."

Questioning eyes briefly met his. "Oh?"

"Not so much a favor, I suppose, as a job."

A grin bloomed and his heart knocked. "A job? Keep talking."

"It's not a huge project, but…Jack's room needs some serious updating. And I've seen your work on your website. So—"

"Really? You checked me out?"

Wes felt his cheeks warm. "My mother did, actually.

At my suggestion, though. Since Mom's idea of redecorating is changing the drapes and carpeting for a fresh version of what's already there." Blythe laughed and his heart knocked again. "So would you be interested?"

"Absolutely. I love doing kids' rooms."

"Good," Wes said on a relieved sigh. "Decorating was Kym's thing, not mine. Even if I had the time. But I think the kid's probably ready to ditch the race car theme his mom did for him when he was six."

"Let me guess—complete with race car bed?"

"You got it. I have no idea what he wants, though."

"Don't worry about it. That's between Jack and me." Another, slyer grin slid across her face. Sly, and teasing, and sexy, even if Wes doubted that the sexy part was intentional. And sexy wasn't quite the right word. Intense? That was closer. He guessed she was the kind of person who fully lived in the moment, relishing it for its own sake. "I assume I have carte blanche to do anything he wants?"

"Short of papering his room with pics of naked women, yes."

This time her laugh was loud enough to make people turn their heads. "I'll take that under advisement." Then her brow knotted. "I'm pretty booked up through March, though—will that be a problem?"

"The kid's already waited a year, I'm sure he can hang on for another six weeks."

She nodded, then pushed her eggs around her plate for a moment before asking, "Does that happen a lot? People coming up to you out of the blue?"

Wondering what brought on the subject switch, Wes said, "Not everyone recognizes me, of course. But yeah. Being accosted is part of the job description. I don't mind," he said to her slight frown. "That's why I did this, after all. To listen. And help, when I can. Although my staff handles most of the actual problem-solving. I sure as hell couldn't do it all myself."

Laughter from her cousins' table momentarily snagged her attention; she slugged back half her orange juice, then met his gaze again. "And Jack…is he okay with sharing you so much?"

Over the years, first with his law practice and then on the campaign trail, Wes had gotten pretty good at hearing what people weren't fully saying. Meaning he immediately sensed more layers to Blythe's question than a simple answer could address…even if he hadn't asked himself the same question a hundred times since taking office. And in those layers he sensed both irritation and genuine concern.

Even so, annoyance spurted through him as well, that she'd ripped the bandage off a festering sore. And by rights, he should have changed the subject, re-covered the sore, not poked at it by saying, "You think I'm neglecting him."

Color bloomed in her cheeks as she picked up her fruit cup, forking through it to spear a honeydew wedge. "Forget it, it's really none of my business—"

"Don't you dare backtrack," Wes said, and her startled gaze shot to his. "Or think you have to spare my feelings. Believe me, I have the hide of a rhinoceros." He snorted. "Makes it harder for people to take a chunk of it. Worse than that, though, are the kiss-ups, people more intent on telling me what they think I want to hear than what I need to hear." He leaned forward, seeing something deep, deep inside those deep blue eyes that plunged right inside him and latched on tight. "So out with it."

Blythe froze, the fruit cup suspended over her plate. Granted, she'd never been one to shy away from a challenge, but did she dare say what she was really thinking?

And how could she do that without backing the man into a corner? And yet, for the child's sake…

Carefully she set down the small glass dish, then lifted her eyes to his. "Fair warning, Wes—saying 'out with it' to me is like waving a red flag in front of a bull."

"Somehow, I figured as much. So?"

She pushed out a sigh. "*Neglect* isn't the right word. Trust me, I know from neglect. That would imply you're deliberately ignoring him, which I know isn't true—"

"But you think Jack sees it that way."

After a moment, she nodded. "From what I've observed, and heard, when I'm around the kids…" The space between her brows puckered. "I think he sometimes feels like he has to fight for your attention. And that could…" She felt her pulse hammering. "It *could* lead to places you don't want him to go."

His own breakfast long since finished, Wes leaned back in the booth, his arms tightly crossed, as though to keep his annoyance from escaping.

"You asked," she said gently.

On a released sigh, he unfolded his arms to prop his wrists on the table's edge, looking out the window for a moment before meeting her gaze again.

"You know this for a fact."

The ache in his voice, the fear…her heart cracked. "That it will happen? No, of course not. That it could? Absolutely."

Their gazes tangled for a long moment. "Speaking from personal experience?"

"Partly," she said after a moment. "And that's all I'm going to say about that. I also have no intention of giving you advice, but from what I've seen…I thought you should know."

"And you think I don't?" Wes lobbed back, his voice

low but his eyes screaming with guilt, with ambivalence. "That I'm so engrossed in this job I'm oblivious to my son's pain?"

"No, Wes, of course not. But—"

"But, what?"

Her hand covered his before she even realized she was doing it. "Redoing his room won't make up for your not being there."

"And maybe that's all I have." He pushed out a rough breath, then seemed to realize they were touching. Slipping his hand out from under hers, he said, "I know this is far from ideal. Especially since this wasn't how things were supposed to pan out. The plan was, if I won, that Jack's mother would be there for him when I couldn't be. The *plan* did not include some texting teenager slamming into her and Deanna on a wet road three weeks before an election I didn't actually think I'd win."

Then he schooled his features in that way men did when they didn't want you to see the torture behind them. *Too late,* Blythe thought as Wes continued. "But I did win. And I'd made promises to those people who put me in office. Not to mention to my wife, who'd been my staunchest supporter through that campaign from hell. Promises I feel very strongly about, that…"

Breathing hard, he shook his head. "I'm between a rock and a hard place, Blythe. And I'm trying my damnedest to find a balance. Jack's hardly fending for himself, with my parents living in the house. And when I'm in Washington I call him every morning to wake him up, Skype every evening before he goes to bed, if I can—"

Wes signaled to the waitress for the check, waving off Blythe's noises about paying for her own breakfast. Check in hand, he stood and called to Jack, who was clearly reluctant to leave Quinn, then faced Blythe again.

"I'm making the best of an impossible situation, even though I know…I know it's not enough." He dug his wallet out of an inside pocket in his coat, tossed some bills on the table before punching his arms through the sleeves. "But what else can I do—?"

"Dad?" Jack came up behind him, his forehead crunched. "You okay?"

Wes turned to smile for his son. "I'm fine. But we need to get going, I've got a ton of reading to get through before I go back tonight."

After they left, Blythe dumped her wadded up napkin on her plate and lowered her head to her hands, feeling her cousins' puzzled gazes boring into her skull.

Yeah. The ride back to St. Mary's should be *really* interesting.

Chapter Three

Between her other work and the wedding plans, it was indeed nearly the end of March before Blythe could slot an appointment to see Jack's room. Six weeks during which she hadn't spoken to Wes except to ascertain whether the project was still a go, since, after that tense little confab in the HoJo restaurant, it seemed prudent to check. She'd also be a big fat liar if she said she hadn't thought of Wes during those six weeks.

A lot. More to the point, a lot more than she should have, considering her who-needs-men? stance of late.

Especially stressed-out, still grieving men, already juggling way too many rings without trying to add a little somethin'-somethin' into the mix. Not that he would, but if he did…

Oh, never mind. Pointless musings were, well, pointless.

As much as possible, she'd steered clear of her nosy cousins as well, having taken her skinny little tush back to

Washington immediately after their return to St. Mary's. Because the newly engaged were even worse than the newly converted, shoving their happiness down your throat in the hopes that you, too, could be saved if only you'd repent. Especially if they sensed you were *thisclose* to seeing the light.

Except having the hots for someone—no point in denying it—was way different than wanting to plight your troth with them. Or to them. Whatever. That she'd done, it didn't take, let's move on. Troth-plighting clearly wasn't her thing.

And it clearly was Wes's. Or had been at one point. And Blythe had no doubt it would be again, some day. Just not with her, she reminded herself as she pulled up that late Thursday afternoon in front of the quasi-colonial five houses down from the inn.

Not huge, but stately all the same. Brick front. White columns. Black shutters. A fitting congressman's abode, she mused, punching the doorbell, clasping her gray mohair wrap to her neck against the biting spring breeze off the water. Bear, Jack's black Lab, started barking; Blythe heard shushing, then the white paneled door swung open, revealing a short, trim older woman in jeans and a floral-appliquéd sweatshirt, her bright red smile welcoming underneath a froth of gray hair that treaded that delicate line between curls and frizz.

"After all the times we've talked on the phone," Candace Phillips said, ushering her inside a black-and-white-tiled entryway with pale blue walls, "it's so nice to finally meet you. The children are in the family room, playing one of those video games. Can I get you something to drink? Should I call Jack?"

"No to both," Blythe said, squatting to pet the exuberant dog, dodging his kisses as she surreptitiously took in the entryway, what she could see of the living and dining rooms. It was weird, considering how often she'd schlepped the kids around, that she'd never actually been inside the house. Which, while reeking of tradition, was warm and tasteful and timeless, the colors and furnishings in perfect balance. She stood and turned to Candace, and the dog bounded back to his young master, skidding on the tile before regaining his footing on the Oriental carpet anchoring the formal dining room table. "At least, not yet for Jack. I want to see his room before I get his take on what he'd like in it."

"Good idea. I'm sure Kym would have seen to the redo long before now, if…"

Candace paused, her lips pressed tight as she scanned the living room, the Wedgwood-green walls a soothing backdrop to the marble fireplace, the pair of white sofas facing each other on another Oriental rug. And yet, pops of a soft purple and a deep coral perfectly complemented the dusty green, keeping the room from being too staid. A room that hadn't been used in a while, Blythe suspected.

"She had a very good eye," Candace said. "Well, I think so. But then, I'm no designer." She blushed. "As I'm sure Wes told you."

Blythe smiled. "Good design is about surrounding yourself with whatever makes you happy. There are far fewer rules than you might think. As long as the home reflects the owners' personalities, it's good. And this is…" Her gaze swept the living room once more. "It's lovely. Really."

Candace beamed, clearly pleased that her obviously much-loved daughter-in-law had passed muster. "It is, isn't it? And that was Kym—warm and embracing, but understated and conservative." She paused. "She and Wes married so young, his father and I…well, we worried. That they didn't know what they were getting into. Silly us," she said with a little laugh, then gave her head a firm shake. "And listen to me, rambling on..." She headed toward the stairs, beckoning Blythe to follow.

"I understand Kym was a huge support to Wes when he ran for office," Blythe said as they started up.

"Oh, my, yes," Jack's grandmother said, half pivoting as she trudged. "In fact, Kym gave Wes the push he needed to throw his hat in the ring."

"Really? It wasn't his idea?"

They reached the landing; Candace bustled to the second door on their right, holding it open for Blythe to pass through. "Yes, of course it was Weston's idea—he'd been thinking about running for Congress for a long time. After all, he'd been on the town council for five years—" which Blythe hadn't known "—but he kept putting off taking that next step. Said the timing wasn't right, that Jack needed to be older. Kym, of course, bless her heart..."

As if realizing where her musings were leading her, Candace turned, tears shimmering in her eyes. "We do what we can," she whispered, "and I know Wes does, but Jack..." She shook her head, as if realizing she'd crossed some boundary she shouldn't have. Instead, she stood aside so Blythe could see the kid's room in all its messy, outgrown glory. "And maybe this will help him find his footing again. Discover who he is now. Am I making any sense?"

"Absolutely," Blythe said, wondering if her own grand-mother—hell, her own *mother*—had been half as intuitive as this woman, then maybe things would have turned out differently for her. "Jack is very lucky to have you around."

Candace's brown eyes popped wide. "Well, aren't you sweet?" Then she sighed. "Bill and I do our best, but we're still poor substitutes for what he lost. Well. I'll let you get to it. I'm in the kitchen if you need me."

After Candace left, Blythe stood in the middle of the

jumbled room, trying to get a feel for it. See what it said to her. A large space, she noticed approvingly. And light-filled. Or would be light-filled once the heavy curtains were axed. Honeycomb shades, she thought, to let in the light and yet give him privacy. The beige wall-to-wall carpeting looked in decent condition, but a couple of fun throw rugs would definitely liven things up. Ditch the little boy race car motifs, replace them with lots of high-tech accents. Something that wouldn't embarrass him when he came home from college, she thought with a smile. An inviting study area in the far corner. Track lighting, maybe, to replace the sucky overhead—

"Bear!" she yelped, laughing, when the dog poked his nose in her bum. "What are you doing, you goofy mutt—?"

"How come you're in here?"

Blythe whipped around, taken aback by Jack's rigid stance, the glower on his face. What would soon be a handsome, swoon-worthy face, she had no doubt, his features already morphing into a facsimile of his father's underneath the surfer-blond hair.

"I'm so sorry, I didn't mean to intrude." Then it hit her, that the radical attitude shift probably had nothing to do with her. "Your dad didn't tell you he'd hired me to help you redecorate your room, did he?" The dog knocked his huge, gleaming head against her palm. Jack glared at the beast as though he'd betrayed him, then turned agitated green eyes to Blythe.

"So that's what you two were talking about? That morning at breakfast? After I left?"

Blythe smiled. "Hatching our sinister plot—yes, we were." Then she remembered. "Your grandmother said 'the children.' Is Quinn here, too?"

"Yeah. She thinks I went to the bathroom." Jack looked around the room, then threw his school-uniformed self on the rumpled little-boy bed, an incongruous image if ever there was one. Then again, incongruity pretty much summed up kids that age, didn't it? Too big to be coddled, not nearly old enough to handle the very grown-up issues that life far too often flung in their faces.

Sure, many kids had it far worse—something she'd told herself over and over at that age, when faced with all the crap she didn't know how to handle, either. But she'd decided a long time ago that nobody got to decide whether somebody's hurt was more or less valid than anyone else's. Or that, given her own experience, there was a kid alive who could do or say anything that would shock her. Or keep her from being his or her champion, if necessary.

"What if I don't want to change anything? I mean—" Jack grabbed a pillow and wadded it under his head "—what if I like it the way it is?"

Blythe's brows lifted. "This wasn't your idea?"

The boy was quiet for a moment, then suddenly sat up, slamming his sneakered feet onto the floor. "I mentioned it *once,* yeah. Like, a year ago. When I thought…" He shook his head, hard, then looked around. "I don't want somebody coming in and changing it around just because. It's *my* room, dammit."

Blythe carefully shifted the pile of clothes on a nearby chair to sit on the edge. "Yes, it is," she said, knowing how it felt to desperately want to hang on to what you knew, even if it hurt. "Which is why I wouldn't dream of getting rid of anything you want to keep. That's not my job—"

"You're right, it's not," the boy shot back, more pain than anger sparking in his green eyes. "Because I thought—"

He slammed his arms across his chest, clamping his jaw shut in an obvious effort to keep a lid on his emotions. Again, Blythe reminded herself that this wasn't about her.

"Because you wanted your father to help?"

After a moment, Jack nodded, and Blythe considered what to say next. "I'm not sure your dad knew where to begin," she finally said. "So since this is what I do for a living, he asked me to get things going. That doesn't mean he can't still be part of it."

Jack's eyes shunted to hers. "He'll probably be too busy."

"Why don't you let me worry about that?" Blythe said, smiling, then pushed through with, "And I promise, you can keep anything you want. Although you might want to think about updating a thing or two—" she pointed to the bed, which got a grunt "—maybe change the wall color?" She glanced up. "Ditch the wallpaper border?"

The boy's eyes followed hers. "I remember when Mom put that up there."

"Yeah? How old were you?"

His mouth twisted. "Six." Then he sighed. "I guess it is kinda little kid-ish."

"Yeah. And judging from what a great job your mom did with the rest of the house, I'll bet she would've changed things here by now, anyway."

Silence bumped between them for a moment or two before he said, "She told me I could paint the walls brown, if I wanted. Before...before she died, I mean."

"We can still do that," Blythe said, aching for his sadness. "We can go to Home Depot, you can pick the color you see in your head—"

"Except I don't want brown anymore."

"Then you can choose something else," Blythe said, feeling like she was playing table tennis. "This is *your* project. I'm only here to make it happen. We can even go shopping together, so you can pick out your new bed and bedding, new accessories, whatever you want. Here," she said, digging in her bag for her tablet and a tape measure. "Let's take some measurements."

Another glare. "Now?"

"No pressure," Blythe said, still digging. Not looking at the boy. "But I'm here, so I might as well." She held out the tape measure. "So we're all ready to go when you are."

Several beats passed before Jack pushed himself off the bed and took the heavy silver measure, weighing it in his hand for a moment like he was half considering chucking it through the window. "What if I want to make the walls four different colors?" he asked, challenging, holding one end of the measure as Blythe stretched out the tape.

"Why not?" she said evenly, glancing over in time to see a smile—complete with baby dimples, God help the women in his future—creep across his cheeks.

They were nearly finished when Candace reappeared, Quinn tagging behind her, the child's wild red hair an absolute affront to her own white polo and khakis, like Jack's. The dog, who'd been dozing in the puddle of light on the carpet, jumped to his feet and wriggle-bounded over to Quinn, as though he hadn't seen her in years.

"We thought the earth had swallowed you up, jeez," Quinn said, then realized Blythe was there. "Blythe! What are you—? Holy cannoli—are you going to do Jack's room?"

Blythe smiled. "We're talking about it."

"Well, talk harder, because—" her expression mildly horrified, she checked out the space "—it is *way* past time this place got a face-lift. I've never said anything before, but dude. Seriously—that *bed?*"

Blythe held her breath. And squelched a laugh. Honestly, except for the red hair, the kid was her mother's clone. Except then Blythe saw the indulgent smile stretch across Jack's face and realized she had nothing to worry about.

Although Mel might. Down what could be far too short a road.

As if reading Blythe's mind, Candace sighed. "Quinn's been so good for Jack," she said in a low voice. "We absolutely love her. But we do *not* let them come up here by themselves. I know how young kids start…experimenting these days. Can't be too careful."

Although, come to think of it, Quinn had vehemently informed them all not long ago that she'd slug any boy who dared tried to pull any of "that funny business." Probably something to do with now knowing that her mother had gotten pregnant at sixteen, an event that had complicated Mel's life no end. Granted, Blythe imagined that Quinn's attitude toward "funny business" would change sooner rather than later, but maybe the road wouldn't be so short, after all.

"With Bear as a chaperone?" she said as the dog wedged between the two of them with a sappy doggy grin on his face. "I think you're good."

To her credit, Candace chuckled. "You may have a point. Listen, would you like to stay for dinner? Quinn's here quite often, anyway, when her mom's on duty at the inn and Ryder's on call. Makes it feel more like a family," she whispered. "Instead of the poor boy being stuck with his grandparents night after night."

"Oh. I'd planned on driving back to the city tonight. And I wouldn't want to put you out—"

"Don't be silly, it's just pot roast, there's plenty. Unless—" Horror streaked across her laugh-lined face. "You're one of those vegetarians or vegans or something?"

Blythe laughed. "Not me. I love pot roast."

"Then it's settled. And this way you wouldn't have to worry about finding dinner so late when you got back, right?"

"Please, Blythe?" Quinn said from the other side of the room. Winsome grin and all. Yes, it irked Blythe that she and April hadn't even known the child existed until a few months ago, that she'd missed all those years when she could have played the doting "auntie," but since she was more comfortable with older kids, anyway, she supposed it was for the best. "Then you could drive me back to Mom's and Ryder's afterward so the Phillipses wouldn't have to."

"Now, honey," Candace said, "you know that's no bother—"

"I'd be delighted to stay," Blythe said. "Thank you." Because as long as Wes wasn't part of the picture, what could it hurt? "What can I do to help?"

"Not a blessed thing. Dinner's all done, and the kids set the table. Come on, children—chore time!"

Blythe and the dog followed the intoxicating pot roast scent—and Candace—downstairs and into the kitchen, an open-concept marvel in off-whites and light pine cabinets opening up to the family room that, like the rest of the house, managed to be classy and unpretentious at the same time. Wes's father, Bill, was watching the news on the big-screen TV, but he stood when the women trooped through, heartily shaking Blythe's hand, his grin as infectious as his wife's.

Not to mention his son's.

And despite the sadness still tingeing everyone's eyes, the trying-too-hard-to-make-everything-normal-for-the-kid's-sake vibes, envy still zinged through her. Because at least they were here for each other, they were trying. In fact, she guessed Wes's parents had put their own lives on hold to take care of their grandson, a sacrifice she sure as heck hadn't witnessed firsthand. So she briefly mourned this family dynamic she'd never had—and doubted she ever would—even as she decided to content herself with stealing a sliver of a life that wasn't hers. Living vicariously was better than not living at all, she supposed.

However, they'd no sooner settled at the round pine table in the kitchen's bay window when the dog lurched to his feet and took off, followed by Jack yelling, "Dad! You said you wouldn't be home until tomorrow," as he streaked from the room.

Good thing she'd donned her big girl panties this morning, that's all she had to say.

"…and Blythe's here, she came to talk about redoing my room, and it's going to be *awesome,* I get to pick out all the new stuff and she said I can keep whatever I don't want to get rid of! Cool, huh?"

Whoa. Dumping his briefcase on his office desk, Wes couldn't decide which was messing with his head more, his son's sounding like an excited six-year-old, or—

"Blythe's here?"

"Yeah." Jack frowned. "She said you arranged it."

The appointment, yes. Her staying for dinner, no. Although, knowing his mother, why was he surprised?

What he definitely was, was dead on his feet. And for sure he didn't know how he felt about seeing, in his kitchen, the woman whose honesty and craziness and soul-searing gaze had haunted his thoughts and dreams for the past six weeks.

And there she was, stuck at the one seat at the table without easy egress, the only woman in the world who could look radiant in gray. She also looked a bit deer-in-headlighty, which in another life he might have found amusing.

Then his mother—glowing, as usual—popped up from the table and bustled toward the cooktop. "Isn't this a nice surprise!" she said, ladling pot roast and veggies onto a plate and bustling back. And a surprise it was, an impetuous decision made two hours ago when he realized the thought of spending the night in his office, which he usually did without complaint, made him want to blow his brains out. He wanted to see his family. His son. Now.

Blythe, however—

She lifted one hand and did a finger wiggle. She might have been blushing. Hard to tell in the candlelight. "Hi."

Loosening his tie, Wes took his seat across the table from her, leaning back slightly when his mother set a plate of food in front of him. Bravely, he met Blythe's gaze. Felt the zing. "Hi," he said, thinking, *Damn.*

Nope, six weeks of not seeing her hadn't done a blessed thing to dampen his…ardor. This was so not good. Because he was so not ready for…ardor. Or anything else. Although he was grateful to see that some of the terror had abated in those blue eyes that, yep, were still doing the same number on his…head that they'd done that morning in the restaurant.

He was attracted to the woman. *Very* attracted. Attracted in that way that makes men do dumb things. Especially men dumb enough to think staying busy was a good way to avoid, you know. Living.

"Your mother invited me to stay for dinner," she said as Wes dug into his food, praying the nourishment would revive him enough to plow through the lengthy bill being discussed on the floor the next day.

"So I see," he said, except he could barely hear himself because Jack was yakking away a mile a minute in his ear.

Wait. Jack yakking a mile a minute?

Forking in a bite of moist, tender beef—his mother did make a mean pot roast—he looked over at his son. Who seemed, if not happy, at least captivated by something that wasn't a video game. Huh.

Just go with it, he thought, returning his gaze to Blythe.

Who was watching his son with an *I got your back, kid* expression Wes found both gratifying and annoying as hell.

As if dinner itself hadn't been bizarre enough, between watching Wes do the whole *Who is this kid?* thing with Jack and trying to ignore the *zzzzap!* to her girl parts every time the man looked at her, afterward ventured dangerously close to *Twilight Zone* territory.

Blythe would have imagined, given Jack's obvious resentment over his father's frequent absences, and his equally obvious excitement that Wes had come home, that the kid would have commandeered Wes's attention for the rest of the evening. Not so. Instead, the moment he'd dispatched the last molecule of caramel sauce from his sundae glass, he pointedly dragged Quinn off to finish up their game. Which, in turn, had produced another flash of that lost look in Wes's eyes before, after thanking his mother for dinner and giving her a kiss on the cheek, he also vanished. Leaving Blythe feeling equally at sea, especially when Candace refused her offer to help tidy up.

"That's my job," Wes's dad said with a wink as he carted over stacked plates from the table. "And I'm sure you wouldn't want to put an old man out of work now, would you?"

And the odd thing was, Blythe thought as she gathered her things, it was clear she would have usurped the older man's position. Because, listening to the couple's easy chatter as they scraped and rinsed the dishes and filled the dishwasher, it was obvious this was one of those little rituals that kept the couple's love alive and kicking. It wasn't what they did, but that they did it together, the act of sharing the moment turning the mundane into the sweet.

Jeez. What had the woman put in that pot roast, anyway? Because this whole cozy-family thing wasn't *her* thing.

Seriously. Sure, she loved hanging with her cousins and all. But they were more like gal pals than relatives, you know? Yeah, yeah, April and Mel kept going on about how they were more like sisters, and Blythe had to admit there'd been the occasional moment during the past several months when she could see where they were coming from. But that didn't mean she was coming from the same place. Or any place, really. Family…that's what other people had.

Some other people, anyway. Hey, from what she could tell, this was one of those things that looked a lot better on paper than it did in practice. Because in her experience, people were far more likely to screw it up than make it work.

At least, people who didn't have decent examples to follow. Say what you will about no man being an island, making connections with other human beings wasn't nearly as innate as "they" would have you believe.

"Why don't you go take a tour of the rest of the house while you wait?" Candace shouted over the grinding of the garbage disposal.

Blythe nodded, even as she wondered, *Wait for what?* A question soon answered when she found the kids in the family room, intent on conquering aliens. Or something.

"Oh. I thought you'd be ready to go," Blythe said to Quinn's back as she slipped on her sweater.

"Mom doesn't get home for another hour," Quinn said, not even missing a beat as her blurred hands commanded the remote. She spared Blythe the sparest of glances, her hair electrified around her shoulders. "When Ryder's not there, Jack's grandpa takes me home around nine."

"What about homework?"

"Did it," she said with a distracted shrug. "So it's cool. Really…" She bit her lip as the green critter on the screen did something apparently awesome, given Quinn's "Take that, suckah!" in response.

Talk about feeling old.

Figuring that self-guided tour was as good a way to waste time as any, Blythe poked around downstairs for a few minutes, even as she realized the house was larger than it appeared. Not ostentatiously so, but definitely not a shack, the formal living room leading into a lovely, large sunroom facing the water. And off to one side, a double-paneled door stood half open to what she assumed was an office or library.

Office, she realized, peeking into the very manly room, all dark wood and striking mid-century art against burgundy walls, a massive wooden desk adjacent to the bay window, a twin to the one in the living room. An add-on, she thought, destroying the colonial's original symmetry but well enough done, from what she could tell. She pushed the door farther open to smile at the ubiquitous leather furniture…her smile fading when she realized Wes was slouched in a corner of the tufted sofa, watching her, amusement dancing in his tired eyes.

"Oops, didn't mean to intrude," she said, stepping back, exactly as he'd expected her to. Even though Wes sensed that her reticence had more to do with her being caught off guard than having breached his privacy.

"You're not," he assured her, even though he definitely felt intruded upon. Had, from the moment he'd seen her sitting at his table. Yes, despite his having initiated the intrusion to begin with by asking her to do Jack's room. Logic had nothing to do with whatever was going on in his brain.

Jack's brush-off after dinner, however, did.

Despite his exhaustion, Wes forced himself to sit forward. To stifle what had to have been his hundredth yawn since he'd arrived home. Not to mention some strange, unsettling impulse to use Blythe's obvious discomfiture to his advantage. Play the power card, in other words.

As if he had clue one how to do that. No, change that: he was as well-versed in charm and manipulation as the next politician. He could even be cunning, if push came to shove. But that wasn't what he was about. Never had been. And if that made him a wuss, too bad.

"I thought you'd gone."

"Can't leave until Quinn and Jack have saved the universe," she said, and Wes chuckled.

"You're returning to D.C. tonight?"

"Actually, since it's so late I might crash at Mel's. Haven't decided yet. And you look like a man who can't believe he's still awake." When he gave her a thumbs-up, she smiled. "So why don't you go to bed?"

"Before my son? That would be beyond pathetic. And why are *you* standing in the doorway?" He waved her inside. "Come keep me company." The yawn finally escaped. "Or at least awake."

"I—"

"You got anything better to do?"

"Here? No."

"Well then?"

Sighing, she entered the library-slash-office to dump her bag and computer on a side table before wriggling out of her sweater, plopping it on top of everything else. "Impressive," she said, taking in the room before bestowing a careful smile in his direction. "You should be nursing a lowball. In cut glass."

"Don't drink," Wes said on a tired smile. "Never did much, but after Jack was born…" He shrugged, then felt one side of his mouth lift. "Makes me hugely unpopular at social events. Although it is reassuring to know the kid isn't going to get into my liquor cabinet while I'm gone. And you're not sitting."

Finally she did, in a wing chair across from him, leaning back with her hands draped loosely over the arms, her legs crossed. But the set to her jaw gave the lie to her relaxed pose. Not that she felt trapped, he didn't think. But she looked obligated to play along when she didn't want to. Part of him wanted to release her from the obligation. Or at least give lip service to it, since he didn't doubt for a moment that if she wanted to leave, she would. And yet, perversely, he wanted her to stay. Just to have someone to talk to who didn't have an agenda.

Then again, maybe she did.

"I take it Jack has some ideas for his room?"

Her lips stretched. Slightly. "We're getting there. At first he didn't want to change anything. Which is understandable," she said gently. "Given the circumstances. Then he said he might want to paint all four walls different colors, but he has no idea what those colors might be. It was a bit like nailing Jell-O to a tree."

"Sounds about right."

"So you're okay with four different wall colors?"

"If that's what he wants, go for it."

"Has he always been this quixotic?"

Wes shook his head, thinking of his son's reaction to him that night. The rejection stung, no doubt about it. "I don't think so. I mean…" He leaned back, his eyes closed, realizing she was once more sucking him into a conversation he wasn't sure he should be having with a virtual stranger. And yet, wanted to.

He opened his eyes, faced Blythe's. Wasn't sure he liked what he saw. Did know, however, that it was weird, seeing her sitting where Kym always had, at the end of a long day, her legs tucked up under her as she laughed, regaling him with stories about their son's antics. There'd always be a cup of tea in her hands, her slender fingers curved around the ceramic, her long, dark hair falling in loose waves over her shoulders, exactly the way it had when she'd been a teenager. As though she'd been caught in time, like a beautiful, delicate insect in amber. As the memory was now, in his head.

"I don't remember Jack's being so moody before. When he was younger, I mean. But then, Kym was around him more than I was. She was the go-to parent. I was..." he sighed "...the auxiliary. I didn't mean it to work out that way," he said to Blythe's slight frown. "It just did."

After a pause, she said, "He wants you to help him with his room, you know."

"Me? I don't know a damn thing about design."

"That's not the point."

No, it wasn't. And he knew it. Knew, too, that whatever problems he and Jack were having were his fault, not the kid's. That, being the grown-up, he was supposed to be able to fix this. That he couldn't—

Frustration trumping exhaustion, Wes heaved himself off the couch, almost wishing he did have that drink. Instead he crossed to the French doors leading to the side yard, shoving them open to let in the damp breeze, soothing against his heated face. "This parenthood gig ain't for wusses," he said, his back to her.

"Precisely why I don't think I'd make a very good mother."

Frowning, Wes turned. "Really?"

"Really. I've finally reached the point where I'm happy with my life. I love what I do. Who I've finally become. What can I say?" She smiled. "Autonomy is the *bomb*."

"And yet you get along so well with Quinn. Jack, too, for that matter."

Something dimmed in her eyes. The truth, Wes suspected. Especially when she said, "Relating to kids doesn't automatically translate into wanting my own. For one thing, I'm not sure I have the courage to be a parent. And for another, shoehorning a child into my life...it wouldn't be fair."

Wes pushed aside the tailored drapery flapping alongside the open window before focusing on Blythe again. "Is that what you think I'm doing? Shoehorning Jack into my life?"

He saw her suck in a tiny breath. "I'm talking about myself. Not you."

"You sure about that?"

She returned his gaze for several seconds, then sighed. "I'm not questioning your skills, I swear. Or how much you love your kid, because that's obvious. But..." Frowning, she briefly rubbed the heels of her hands against the chair arms before clutching the ends. "In some respects, I see myself in Jack. At that age, I mean. So I empathize with him. What he's feeling."

Curiosity overrode his reaction to her first comment—that she had every right to question his skills, since God knows he did. "You lost your mother, too?"

One side of her mouth hitched up. "The question is if I ever really had her. But my father...yeah. He removed himself from my life when I was a little older than Jack." Sympathy flooded her eyes. But for whom? "I *know* you haven't abandoned Jack, and my mother's continued detachment in no way compares to what Jack's suffered. But to a child, I'm not sure the loss feels that much different—"

"Bly-ythe!"

At Quinn's yell, Blythe stood and called back, "In Jack's dad's office," then gathered her things again. "It's obvious you're trying to make the best of a complicated situation,

Wes. And if I was smart," she said on another slight smile, "I'd simply do my job—if you still want me to, I don't think Jack would care one way or the other—and keep my big mouth shut. But it kills me to see him hurting so much—"

Wes grabbed her hand, clearly startling her. And himself. "Then help him. If you're seeing something I can't, for God's sake, *help him.*"

It clearly took a moment for her to find her voice. "But... there are therapists," she said, reclaiming her hand.

"And he's clammed up with every one I've taken him to. And he trusts you—"

"Ready!" Quinn burst through the door, Jack right behind her.

"Good." Blythe jerked away to dig inside her gargantuan purse. "Here, Jack—" Her smile brighter than necessary, she handed the boy her business card. "Anytime you're ready to talk ideas, give me a call. Leave a message if you get my voice mail, I'll get right back to you." Then she smiled up at Wes, and he saw *I'll do what I can* in her eyes.

A cautious promise though it may have been.

Seconds later, they were gone. His hand clamped around the back of his neck, Wes crashed back onto the leather couch, releasing a huge sigh of what should have been relief—that maybe, somehow, Blythe *could* mitigate some of the yearning, the distrust in Jack's eyes that seemed to intensify every day.

Except...by asking Blythe to help heal the ever-widening gulf between him and his son, he'd also given her easier access to his life.

And, astoundingly, his heart.

So, that sigh? Relief, no. Sheer terror, however...

Bam.

Chapter Four

"So did you and your mom pick out your junior brides-maid dress yet?"

Quinn, who normally chattered like a squirrel to anyone who'd listen—or not—had been uncharacteristically sub-dued on the drive from the Phillipses house. An only child's need for downtime to recharge after being social all day, Blythe had initially assumed, all too clearly remembering her own preteen years. But after ten minutes of the child's brain waves crackling between them, she'd decided that wasn't it. Although directly asking, "Is something wrong?" would in all likelihood get a "No, I'm fine," in response. Or an eye roll. So Blythe took a more oblique approach.

Especially since she needed to talk about something, anything, to take her mind off Wes's plea to do whatever she could for Jack. And by extension, him. The very real worry in his eyes—sucked her right in, it did. Maybe she'd finally accepted that saying "no" on occasion didn't make her mean, unfeeling or, according to one jerk she'd briefly dated, a frigid bitch. But she was incapable of turning her back on a hurting child. Not when she knew what that felt like—

"Yeah, we did," Quinn pushed out on a sigh.

"What's it look like?"

"Blue. Ruffly. I look like a baby in it but Mom loves it, so whatchagonna do?"

Thinking of her own dress—also blue, also ruffly, something Blythe wouldn't have willingly put on her body in a million years—she smiled. "You're a good kid—"

"Can I tell you something?"

Intuiting that the conversation was about to sharply veer from horrid wedding attire, Blythe glanced at the girl, slumped in her seat.

"Sure," she said lightly. "What's going on?"

In the months since the cousins' reunion, Quinn had quickly figured out that she could vent to Blythe or April without dragging her own mother—along with Mel's inclination toward overreacting—into it. And Mel, apparently, was more than cool with letting her cousins share the load that was her über-smart, verging-on-drama-queen daughter. Apples, trees…'nuff said.

"I'm worried about Jack," Quinn said, and Blythe thought, *Why am I not surprised?* Especially given her younger cousin's propensity for picking up when something wasn't right…an intuition that had been on full alert well before the secrets surrounding her birth had come roaring to the surface the September before. If anything, that event seemed to have left the child even more sensitive to changes in the mental atmosphere.

"Worried?"

"Yeah. He's been acting weird lately."

"Weird, how?"

"Like...I don't know. Like one minute he's okay, and we get along like we always do, and the next minute he practically bites my head off. Only before I even have a chance to get mad, then he's okay again."

"That must be exhausting."

"You're telling me. It's like...what's that story where the crazy doctor has like two personalities, one good and one bad?"

"Dr. Jekyll and Mr. Hyde?"

"That's it. Mom and I watched it one Halloween. Seriously strange movie."

Blythe chuckled, then sobered. "I take it this is something new, then?"

"Newish. I mean, when Jack and I first met, he'd get all mopey about his mom sometimes, but I could usually kid him out of it, you know? But this seems...I don't know. Like he goes someplace way deep inside himself and gets mad when I try to follow."

"I think everybody feels that way sometimes," Blythe said carefully, not wishing to put her own concerns about the boy on a ten-year-old.

"This is different," Quinn said, giving her head a quick shake. "Especially since..."

They pulled through the black wrought-iron gates leading to Ryder's parents' magnificent waterfront house, then around to the caretaker's cottage at the back of the property, where Mel and Ryder were temporarily living until they found a house in town they both liked. "Especially since, what?" Blythe prompted.

"Ohmigosh, Jack would kill me if he knew I was saying anything, but..." Her gaze touched Blythe's. "I'm not the only one he snaps at—he's been doing it to kids at school, too. And at first—well, since I've been there, I mean, I have no idea what went on before—the other kids gave him a wide berth because of his mom, you know? But now they're getting tired of it. Never knowing if he's going to give them attitude or whatever. And I'm afraid one day, something bad's going to happen."

The Lexus's tires crunched the gravel in front of the cottage, crouched underneath a stand of loblolly pines, before she parked alongside Mel's new Toyota Camry. "What does Jack say?"

Quinn snorted. "Oh, like he's going to listen to me? Whenever I ask him what's wrong, he tells me to mind my own business."

"So his dad and grandparents don't know about any of this?"

"You're kidding, right? I mean, Jack's my best friend. And when he's not being crazy, he's totally cool. But I'm telling you, he's getting on my last nerve."

"Did you tell him you don't like it when he's acting like that?"

"Only like five million times. Except he only gets madder and says nobody's forcing me to hang out with him. If I don't like it, I can leave anytime I want."

Blythe looked at her younger cousin's profile, her jaw set in a way that reminded her so much of her mother Blythe almost smiled. "And what do you say when he does that?"

"Nothing. Because I know he doesn't mean it."

"You're sure about that?"

Slowly, Quinn nodded. "It's this look in his eyes, like, I don't know. He's daring me or something." She looked at Blythe, a forty-year-old soul stuck in a ten-year-old body. "He's acting like he wants to push me away, but if you ask me, I think he's just mad. Or confused." She pressed a hand to her chest. "I've been there, I know."

"And I'm guessing you haven't told your mother."

Another snort. "No way. Because she'd tell me to write

him off, that I don't need—" she made air quotes "—*complications* like that in my life. That I don't need *people* like that in my life. That I'm way too young for that crap. I mean, crud. Except for one thing, hello? Was I the poster child for complications, or what? And for another, if I did leave, Jack wouldn't have *any* friends."

Not for the first time blown away by her little cousin, Blythe refocused out the windshield. "Your mom's right, though. In a way." Her gaze returned to the girl. "Your loyalty is commendable, but you're still only a kid. It's not your responsibility to fix Jack. And if there's even a *suggestion* that he might hurt you—"

"Ohmigosh ! No! Never!"

"You're sure?"

"Yes, Blythe. I'm sure. And I know it's not up to me to fix him. Doesn't mean I can't stick by him while he's going through whatever he's going through. Right?"

"Right." Blythe reached over and gently tugged Quinn's curls. "Your mama raised one amazing kid, you know that?"

"Which she never, ever lets me forget," Quinn muttered, and Blythe laughed. Then she frowned.

"So, question—is there a specific reason why you're telling me this?"

Suddenly, earnest blue eyes lanced hers. "I just thought maybe, if, you know, the opportunity presented itself, you could mention it to his dad?"

It was obvious Quinn was truly worried about her friend. And melodramatics aside, she'd never known the kid to stretch the truth so far it snapped. But honestly— what was up today with everyone asking her to intervene?

"That could be tricky, sweetie. Since, for one thing, it's hearsay—"

"Because you didn't hear Jack say any of this yourself?"

"Exactly. And even if I did mention it, and Jack's dad believed me, and brought up the subject with Jack, Jack's bound to know it came from you. That you ratted on him. And that could very possibly destroy your friendship."

"So you won't do it?"

Wes's earnest, pleading hazel eyes flashed in front of her. As if on a damn screen. "I didn't say that. But you need to be aware of the potential consequences. What this might cost you."

"And what's the point if the friendship's based on a lie, anyway?"

Blythe sighed. "Have you thought about saying something to his dad yourself? Or his grandparents?"

"We don't have that kind of relationship," the kid said, and Blythe thought, *And I do?* "I mean, yeah, his grandmother is really nice and all, but it's not like we're ever alone, for one thing. Or that she'd take me seriously, anyway. And his dad's never there. And when he is, he's totally distracted."

Tears welled up in the girl's eyes, and Blythe felt like her heart was being crushed. "I know this sounds crazy, like *I'm* crazy, but I'm really scared for Jack. I'm afraid he's going to do something boneheaded one day because he's not thinking straight. Or he's angry, or whatever. And I know it's lame, putting you in the middle like that, but I don't know what else to do."

Blythe looked out her windshield for a moment. To have Jack's dad, and now this kid Blythe loved more than she loved her shoes, basically ask her the same thing within twenty minutes… Brother. Even so, alerting Wes to her intuition, agreeing—even if only silently—to help Jack, didn't translate to ratting on him. "And how do you expect me to go about this?"

"I have no idea," Quinn said, twisting around to lug her

backpack off the backseat. "That's why you're the grown-up." Straightening, she scrubbed her cheek, then sniffed. "But *promise* you'll do something. Okay?"

"Okay. I promise," Blythe said. "On one condition."

"Don't make me tell Mom, Blythe, please——"

"Sorry, but I'm not about to put my butt on the line with this unless you do. I'll be there with you, if you want, but this is too big to keep your mother out of the loop."

More tears bloomed. "And if she makes me give him up?"

"We'll work it out, sweetie. I swear. But ultimately... that's her call."

Quinn stared at Blythe for a long moment, then shoved open the car door and clambered out to slam the door behind her, her curls bouncing against her back as she clomped up the walk to the cottage.

Yet another reason, Blythe thought as she backed out of the drive, why—as much as she adored her younger cousin—she couldn't imagine doing this full time. Because the thought of facing her younger self every day made her very, very tired.

An hour and a half later—having decided that staying at Mel's would not be wise, considering Quinn's mood—Blythe unlocked the door to her cozy second-floor apartment over her office/studio in Alexandria, Virginia, close enough to D.C. to be convenient, far enough away to be affordable. She loved the charming, Civil War–era house she'd snatched up at a bargain price two years before, flanked on either side by its equally charming cousins on a brick-sidewalked, tree-lined street in the quaint little suburb. Heaven knows the house would be a work-in-progress forever, but as long as she made the mortgage payments at least it was *her* work-in-progress.

Blythe shucked off her heels and wandered into her living room—turquoise walls, original wooden floors, two huge windows partially obscured by a bodacious, modesty-preserving plane tree—where she finally checked her cell. Which had buzzed no less than four times on the drive back. She checked her voice mail—one from April, about table decorations, another from a client needing to reschedule. And one each from Mel and Wes.

Sighing, Blythe called Mel first. Who had not only flown off the handle but had apparently zipped around the block a time or six.

"I want you to tell me *exactly* what Quinn said about Jack. And why did she come to you, anyway, and not me?"

"Working backward, listen to yourself and I think you'll have your answer." Although could we hear a "Yes!" that Quinn had confided in her mom? "As for the first...what did she say?"

Mel basically reiterated what Quinn had told Blythe, that Jack's "weirdness" was alienating the other kids at school, that she worried about him.

"Then you know as much as I do," Blythe said. "Really. I told her she had to let you in the loop, though. For what it's worth."

"Yeah, she said that, too." A pause. "Thank you. Of course now I have no idea what to do. I mean—should I tell her they can't hang out anymore? Except at school, obviously. Although I suppose we could homeschool again..."

"You really think that would work?"

"It would be harder now that she's older, but we'd manage."

"Not talking about homeschooling, birdbrain." When Mel sighed, Blythe said, "This was exactly what she was afraid of, Mellie. That you'd try to break up their friendship."

"She's only ten. And I am her mother. It's my duty to protect her—"

"Of course it is, sweetie. But she's also your spawn. She might obey you on the surface—"

"But make my life a living hell in the meantime?"

Blythe chuckled. "You said it, not me."

Her cousin released another long, heavy breath. "So what should I do?"

"Oh, *now* you want me to be bossy?" she said, laughing, thinking back to when they were kids and her two younger cousins made no bones about how she made them nuts, ordering them around. They had no idea, of course—and neither had she, frankly—how much she thrived on that semblance of control all those years when she'd felt virtually powerless—

Her phone signaled another call coming through. She quickly checked it—Wes, again. As if Mel could read her mind, she said, "Quinn said she asked you to talk to Wes."

"She did. In fact, he's trying to get through now. Listen, I can't tell you what to do. But if it makes you feel any better, I grilled Quinn pretty hard about Jack, and I didn't hear any major alarm bells. Not as far as she's concerned, I mean. I also didn't get any scary vibes when I talked with him tonight. And they're never alone, right? I mean, either you or April or his grandparents are always around—"

"I know, I know, but…" Another huge sigh. "Fine, I'll let things ride. For now. But you'd better tell Mr. Congressman I'm keeping an eagle eye on his son, because if he hurts my kid—"

"He's not going to do that, Mel."

"And you know this, how?"

Not for the first time, Blythe wondered why she'd never told her cousins more about those "missing" years after they stopped coming to St. Mary's every summer. And for several years before that, to be honest. Heaven knows there'd been plenty of opportunity to fess up, what with Mel's producing this kid none of them had known about and April's revelation that her first marriage had been about convenience, not passion. But how could Blythe admit that all those summers she'd lorded it over them, pretending to be the "cool" one, she'd actually been a hot mess? That she'd done some things—okay, a lot of things—she not only regretted, but would have probably resulted in Mel's not letting *her* anywhere near her daughter?

Or so she'd reasoned during that testing period of their renewed relationship. Reasoning that made even less sense now than it did then. What was past, was past, and it was long past time she come clean.

Or at least start the process.

"Because I've been there, sweetie," she said. "Or close enough. And I know the only person he's a danger to right now is himself." For now, that would do. "And I need to call Wes back, so I've got to go."

She disconnected the call, redialing Wes before she chickened out, even as dread congealed like lard in the pit of her stomach.

Because as hard as it might be to reveal her tale of woe to the two women who loved her best, telling it to some man who didn't know her at all—and for whom she had the hots, alas—would be infinitely harder. And more embarrassing. But in order to do what everyone on the damn planet seemed to want her to do, she had no choice.

The next night, Wes took the Metro—only two stops—then walked in the drenching spring rain to the hole-in-the-wall Italian joint Blythe had suggested. Far enough away from the Capitol not to be crawling with interns, she'd said with a weary laugh. The kind of perpetually

crowded, noisy place where nobody would pay attention
to them. Not that paparazzi-haunting was much of an issue
for him. Outside of his district, nobody knew Wes Phillips
from squat. Hell, few people on the Hill even knew who
he was. Which was fine with him. He was here to make
a difference—clichéd though the concept might be—not
to gain notoriety.

Even if he was beginning to realize that it was virtually impossible to make that difference while remaining
under the radar.

Garlic-laced warmth blasted him when he pushed open
the door, easing the knot in his chest. He immediately spotted Blythe, seated in a booth near the back and perusing the
menu, a glass of red wine in her right hand. She glanced
up at his approach, the dim lighting softening her features.
But not the nervousness in her eyes.

"Sorry I'm late," he said, slinging his wet raincoat on
the hook at the end of the booth.

"You're not. My appointment finished up early and I
didn't want to go back home."

He slid across the red vinyl seat opposite her, shoving
his sopping umbrella into the far corner. "Home being…?"

"Alexandria."

"Apartment?"

"House. Small," she added, holding her other hand a
mere four or so inches away from the wineglass. "But
since I work out of it, I can take a lot of the expenses off
my taxes."

"Very wise," Wes said, his gaze flicking over the menu,
even though he already knew what he wanted…ah, yes,
there it was. "How's the lasagna?" he asked, as he tried
to shove aside the weirdness of sitting with a woman in a
restaurant. A woman who was not Kym.

"To die for," the not-Kym three feet in front of him said.

"As is everything else. Trust me, you can't go wrong with anything on the menu—"

"Miss Blythe!" A tiny, heavily accented waiter shuffled over to lay a generously laden breadbasket in front of them, his white apron tied practically underneath his armpits. A huge smile shoved his enormous ears into another dimension. "Is it really you?"

"Gianni!" Laughing, she opened her arms, half standing to give the old guy a hug. "I can't believe you're still here! How *are* you?"

Still grinning, Gianni shrugged. "Eh, you know me, I don't complain. But I was just saying to Frankie, how we hadn't seen you in a while."

He shifted, shouting, over the tangle of conversation, clattering dishes and a faint thread of tacky Italian music, "Frankie! Look who's here!" A moment later Blythe was exchanging hugs with a second, somewhat younger waiter with dyed black hair. Blythe quickly introduced Wes as a "client," then they ordered their dinners and both waiters vanished into the packed restaurant, allowing the pleasant din to settle back around them.

"I'm beginning to see why you recommended the place," Wes said, choosing a piece of garlic bread from the basket.

Blythe ripped apart a breadstick, dunking the doughy end in the saucer of warm, basil-laced olive oil between them. "And you haven't even tasted the food yet."

"How'd you find it?"

"My ex and I used to come here a lot," she said with a slight shrug, taking another bite of the breadstick. "So I stayed away for a while. After we split, I mean. Tonight… I don't know. Just felt like time to come back. Part of my own twelve-step program to stop letting my past push me around."

Their food arrived—his lasagna, her chicken Marsala.

Wes watched her dig in to her food as she'd done at the Howard Johnson's that morning. "You should tell me where they hold meetings," he mumbled, his fork slicing through layers of tender pasta and tomato-sauce-infused cheeses. When her eyes cut to his, he sighed, then lowered his gaze back to his plate. "There are still places I can't bring myself to go back to. TV shows I can't watch, music I can't listen to…"

At her silence, he lifted his gaze to hers again, to find so much sympathy there his chest constricted. Not pity, though. Compassion. Understanding. "I can imagine," she said, then took a sip of her wine. "Be kind to yourself, though. Don't let other people make you feel like you have to rush things to make *them* feel better."

Wes smiled. "She said, vehemently."

"Sorry. Sore spot."

"Your marriage?"

"The disaster formerly known as, yes. Although the pain…it's different of course. For me, the reminders made me more angry than sad. At myself, more than anything."

"Why yourself?" At her hesitation, Wes waved his fork and refocused on his food. Which was more than living up to her praises. "Sorry, I know we're here to talk about my son, not you—"

"No, it's okay." Blythe sagged against the booth seat, the wine in her hand—the key to her openness, maybe? "Because it's all of a piece, isn't it? The reminders pissed me off because I kept making the same mistakes. Kept handing over my trust to somebody else instead of keeping it right here." She gently knocked her fist against her chest, then shook her head. "Never again," she said with a tiny snort, then leaned forward to take another bite.

"Never again, what?"

"What? Oh. Give someone that kind of power over me."

"I take it by 'someone,' you mean 'a man.'"

"Pretty much, yeah. If I don't let anyone in, they can't very well walk out on me, can they? So how is it?" she said, nodding toward his plate.

In style, in manner, Blythe couldn't have been more different from Kym. But although Wes didn't know Blythe well, he'd seen and heard enough to suspect that, like Kym, Blythe wasn't inclined to ration her heart. Except now he suspected that repeated abuse of her giving nature had bruised that heart, lacerated her trust. And realizing that, it took Wes several seconds before his jaw muscles relaxed enough for him to speak.

"Amazing," he finally got out. "I'll have to remember this place. Jack would love it." When she seemed to focus more intently than necessary on her meal, he leaned forward. "I meant what I said the other night. About wanting you to help him. If you can."

"I know," she said, sitting back. "Although, frankly, I'm still a little surprised."

"About what?"

Her lips tilted. "Considering you made it pretty clear that morning in Howard Johnson's that I'd already said more than I should have? Why the sudden change of heart?"

Those deep blue eyes, even darker in the dim light, spoke volumes. "Maybe not so sudden," Wes said, and her brows lifted. He took a sip of his iced tea, frowning slightly at the glass when he set it back on the table. "In any case..." He met her eyes again. "You're the first person with the guts to not tiptoe around, afraid to say something that might upset me." One side of his mouth hiked up. "So my guess is you're more concerned about making sure my kid's okay than ruffling my feathers. And while in some ways that pisses me off no end, it's also admirable as hell."

Another tiny smile flicked across her mouth. "Not that

either was my goal, but I suppose it's good to know some-body appreciates my…forthrightness."

"You don't have much of a filter, do you?"

She laughed. "Sure I do. Even if it leaks at inopportune times." Then she sobered. "But you're right. I do care about Jack. Same as I care about all kids."

At that, something in her voice, her eyes, told him she was still playing her cards close to her chest, even though it had been her suggestion that they meet tonight.

"And yet, you don't think you're mother material?"

"With my luck, I'd get a kid exactly like me. And that, my friend, is a very frightening thought." Before he could push for details, however, she said, "So I'm curious—why didn't you bring Jack here to live with you? After you got elected, I mean?"

"Actually, that had been the plan. Originally. We—Kym and I—had discussed finding someplace to sublet, maybe out in the 'burbs. Putting Jack in school here. But after… the accident, I realized I would have had to hire a full-time housekeeper, since my dad's business in St. Mary's wouldn't allow my parents to relocate. So between the extra expense and saddling my son with a stranger, letting him stay in St. Mary's seemed like the lesser of two evils. If I'd brought him here, he still wouldn't have had me. Not very much, in any case. And he wouldn't have had anything else he knew, either."

She eyed him for a long moment, then gave a short nod. "So where *do* you live when you're here?"

"Actually…I have a cot in my office."

Her brows shot up. "Your office? You mean, in the Capitol? Get out!"

"I'm not the only one. It was that or share space with some of my colleagues in the equivalent of a frat house for grown-ups. Did that in college, have no desire to re-live the experience."

"I don't suppose you considered, uh, backing out of the race?"

"Actually I did. Briefly. Except the election was only three weeks after the accident, for one thing. And for an-other, I knew that's not what Kym would have wanted. Even though…"

"What?"

"Not a single poll gave me a lead. An independent run-ning against an incumbent? It was insane, frankly, to even think I could win. That I did…well, I have to wonder if at least some of those votes weren't out of pity."

Blythe frowned. "You really believe that?"

"I don't *not* believe it. In any case, how could I not see it through? Try to keep the promises I made to all those people who, for whatever reason, voted for me? And I guess, because I needed to believe this, too, that Jack would want…" He felt his throat get tight. "That he'd want what his mother wanted. That he'd jump on the bandwagon right along with me. It was never my intention to let ambition alienate me from my son, Blythe. I swear." The table edge bit into his forearms when he pressed against it. "I can't simply walk away from this, as I'm sure you understand. But that doesn't mean my son doesn't come first. And al-ways will."

Blythe had long suspected that when she finally shucked this mortal coil, the listed cause of death would be "Brain explosion from thinking too hard." Although, since she was still here after the sleepless night from hell, clearly her skull was made of Kevlar. Or Tyvek, maybe.

Because between Wes's request the day before, and Quinn's revelation, and Mel's near flip-out, and Wes's now looking at her like she was some freaking holy woman with the answer to the riddle of life, and—to add to the merriment—several decidedly *un*holy thoughts elbowing through the crowd…

Damn. It was like Mardi Gras in there. All she needed was beads.

Gianni cleared their empty dinner plates, handed them dessert menus, shuffled off. Dessert she could handle. Especially since that, at least, required no thought. Or emotional investment. As opposed to a certain congressman's impassioned defense of what some might see as an untenable situation.

"I know he does, Wes," she said evenly, laying down her menu. "Which is why…"

His head still lowered to the menu, Wes raised his eyes. "Why, what?"

"Choose your dessert first."

He gave her a weird look, but looked at the menu again. "O-kaay…how's the tiramisu?"

"I've heard good things. But I'm a cannoli gal."

Wes signaled to Gianni, who reappeared, took their dessert orders and the menus, and disappeared again. Then Wes leaned back in the booth, his arm slung across the back. "Desserts chosen. Well?"

Mule-headed contractors, prima donna clients, unexpected structural issues…those, she could handle with one arm tied behind her back. But now, looking into Wes's eyes—the eyes of a man who only wanted to do his best, both by his son and by the people he served—she felt a knot swell at the base of her throat. A knot that signaled something really, really bad.

"Well…" She picked up her dessert fork, twiddled it in her fingers. "If you hadn't called me, I would have called you." When he frowned, she said, "Since Quinn asked me to run interference."

"About what?"

"Apparently Jack's been acting weird at school. And to her."

"What do you mean, weird?"

"Losing it over virtually nothing. Being moody. Snapping at her, and other kids, out of the blue."

He held her gaze for several seconds, his pulse ticking in his right temple. "Are you sure?"

"Obviously, I only know what she's told me. But I don't see any reason for her to make it up." Blythe felt her mouth pull sideways. "She might attract attention, but she doesn't seek it."

"No," Wes said, dropping his arm from the booth's back and curling forward, his hands fisted in front of his mouth. "She doesn't."

"And as it was," Blythe added, "she told *me* because she didn't want to tell her own mother, because she was afraid Mel wouldn't let her see Jack anymore. Although she did. Tell Mel, I mean. Don't worry," she said to Wes's darkened expression, "I talked Mel down. For now, anyway."

Gianni brought their desserts. Wes stared at his for several seconds before picking up his spoon. "If that's true, why hasn't the school said anything?"

"I assume because things haven't gotten out of hand."

His worried gaze lanced hers. *"Yet."*

"Yeah. In fact…hate to say it, but truth be told my initial reaction wasn't much better than Mel's. I love Quinn like my own. If Jack hurts a single hair on her head…"

"There will be hell to pay."

She pointed her fork at him, then said, "So you believe me?"

"Did you think I wouldn't?"

"It's not something a parent wants to hear. Especially someone—"

"In my position. Got it."

Blythe sighed, aching for him. "For what it's worth, Quinn didn't want to tell me, either, because she didn't want to get Jack in trouble, and she knows he already has issues. Except she was scared he'd get in trouble, anyway, and then she wouldn't be able to help him. But the minute he actually gets physical with one of the kids—"

Wes held up a hand to stop her, then pushed out a sigh as it crashed back to the table. And Blythe wrapped her fingers around his, only half registering that he returned her clasp. "Quinn made me promise to tell you."

His gaze bored into hers. "Before she gets hurt, you mean."

"Before *anyone* gets hurt." Reluctantly, Blythe removed her hand. "Including you. You've got plenty to deal with," she said, getting a tight little smile in response. "But as I said the other night, I know firsthand how these scenarios can play out. And it's not pretty."

His spoon set down, Wes pushed away his tiramisu. And watched her, waiting, the frustration hardening his features, cracking her heart a little more. Reminding her why she was here.

She blew out a long breath. "As I started to say last night, my situation wasn't the same as Jack's. What you and Jack have gone through…" She swallowed. "But at least he has one parent who cares. And a support system, which I didn't. Not for a long time. And no," she said, biting off the end of her cannoli, "my cousins don't know. Or rather, they only know what I chose to tell them. But the point is, I know what it feels like when your world implodes, when you feel abandoned, whether or not you actually are. And it makes you do some pretty stupid stuff."

He gave her another one of those long, assessing looks. "How stupid?"

She pushed his tiramisu back toward him. "This might take a while, so you might as well fortify yourself...."

He gave her another of those long, assessing looks.

"How much?"

She out just enough to hold her attention. "To a night owl like you—like, as much as well to the yourself."

Chapter Five

The rain had stopped by the time they'd finally finished dinner—or rather, Blythe had finished her story—leaving the air cool and sweet-smelling, the streets still glistening. They'd walked to the Metro station, side by side but not close, Wes's umbrella tapping the wet sidewalk as Blythe gave him space to process what she'd told him. About her mother's marrying her father to spite her grandmother, who'd owned the large waterfront house not far from his own in St. Mary's, and because Blythe's mother had been pregnant with her. That, as far as she could tell, her parents had never really loved each other. Or her, for that matter, she'd said with a shrug that belied the pain she still obviously felt. A pain he couldn't imagine, frankly, making Wes more grateful than ever for his parents, even as crazy as they'd made him at times through the years.

"Took my parents twelve years to admit their mistake," Blythe had said, "by which time I'd pretty much learned to rely on myself."

Even so, the damage had been done, so that by the time her father left for good—she'd said she never heard from him again—she found herself acting out more and more in an apparently vain bid to get her mother's attention. She'd spoken dispassionately enough about the cutting and shoplifting, the dabbling in drugs and early sexual exploration, but with both regret for those lost years as well an almost contradictory determination to keep them lost.

And then along comes some stranger's kid who brings the whole sordid mess right back to the surface.

Upon reaching the entrance to the station, they both stopped, oblivious to the other passengers coming and going, the traffic hissing through the leftover wetness on the street. Wes was bone-weary, God knew, and faced a busy next few days before spring recess. But Blythe's reliving of her past that night had clearly cost her at least some of her hard-won peace. And since that loss was in some measure due to her concern for his son, Wes didn't feel right about leaving her. Not yet.

As if reading his mind, she gave him a small smile, her eyes—in the darkness, the same deep blue as the night sky—heavy with what her confession had cost her. "I'm sure in the long run, Wes, he'll be fine."

A breeze toyed with one of her long earrings; Wes had to stop himself from letting his fingers follow its path along her cheek. From giving her the comfort she was clearly trying to give him. From giving in to something he didn't think she'd appreciate, in the long run.

"Why do you think that?"

"Because he *is* getting the attention I sure as hell never got. And eventually he's going to realize it. That age—it's rough even when things are copacetic. Hormones suck."

Didn't they just? Wes thought, leaning against the railing bordering the Metro entrance. Bad enough he was über-protective by nature, but combined with being close to a woman with so much to give and—in her head, anyway—no one to give back to her...

"I take it you got over the self-destructive behavior?"

After a moment, she nodded, then leaned against the wet railing as well, her hands fisted in the pockets of her long, lightweight sweater. In her heels she was nearly as tall as he was. Kym had been short. Sturdy. Like a bright little sparrow—

"But I had help," Blythe said. "In the eleventh grade, art was the only elective available. Which I did not want to take because my mother was—is—an artist. So, you know, I'd hang myself rather than follow in her footsteps. But I took my sullen ass to class, anyway, and the teacher—Miss Morehouse—had my number by the end of that first week." She smiled. "Man, it was like the woman could see into my soul. Not only did she suspect I had talent—and refused to let me get away with producing crap when she knew I could do better—but she suckered me into helping her after school. Giving me something to focus on besides myself."

"She paid attention to you, in other words."

"Yeah. Just because I existed. Imagine that." Her laugh was soft. Husky. "In any case, eventually I figured out she was actually on my side, so little by little I opened up to her. And at some point she suggested I check out this website for kids who were looking for someplace to anonymously talk about whatever was bugging them. Of course, my initial reaction was, Why would I want to join the losers? But eventually my curiosity got the better of me. And guess what I discovered? That I wasn't the only teenager in the world with problems!" Another laugh. "Although, naturally, I didn't want to admit I was 'like that.' But I kept going back, anyway. Because it was helping."

Wes fought the urge to take her hand. "Your father really dropped out of your life?"

"He really did. I don't even know where he is."

"I suppose you could find him if you wanted to."

"Then, again, he could find me, too."

This said with the fortitude of a woman refusing to let the abandonment derail her, even as the child's pain still threaded through her words. "And your mother?"

"She is who she is," Blythe said with another shrug. "We do talk, occasionally, and I know she cares about me, in her own way. But I've reconciled myself to the fact that we'll never be close."

"I'm sorry," Wes said on an exhale.

"Yeah. Me, too." She shifted, folding her arms over her ribs. "In any case, at Miss M's urging, I started talking to my counselor, who put me in touch with a school therapist. And I began to realize that ultimately I was responsible for my own happiness, that blaming other people was counterproductive. And that there *were* people who cared. Like them. And my cousins. Those summers in St. Mary's—nobody knows what a lifeline those were. Yeah, my grandmother was crazy, but Mel and April..." This time, the smile bloomed full-out. "I love those guys. Always will. Heck, if it hadn't been for them...I don't even want to think about what I might have done."

Wes turned, ostensibly looking out at the street, thinking his request the night before hadn't come from out of left field nearly as much as it might have seemed. Even if it had seemed so at the time. "And the website?"

"That was pretty much after Mel and April and I stopped coming to St. Mary's. Again, a lifeline that saved my butt. Once I got over myself enough to accept it, anyway. But it's true—knowing you're not the only person going through hell goes a long way toward helping you find your way out of it. And corny as it sounds, I found myself through my art. Started to, anyway. And once I did, the destructive behaviors pretty much stopped on their own. Except for…"

When she looked away, Wes prompted, "Except for?"

She sighed, then gave him a warning look at odds with her smile. "Relationships. Despite a boatload of psych courses in college, I kept looking to guys to 'complete' me. Or make me feel worthy. Something. Kept up the pattern right up to and including my marriage. Wasn't until that fell apart that I finally got it through my head that no one else is going to make me whole. And I made a promise to myself never again to fall into old, pointless patterns."

"So you haven't been in a relationship since your marriage ended?"

"Honey, I haven't even been on a date."

"Wow."

She tilted her head. "Have you?"

"Well, no. But that's different."

A tiny, sucked-in breath preceded a long sigh. "Of course it is," she said softly, apology cradling her words. "Although, in either case—" another sigh "—to hop back into another relationship before you're healed…"

Another *ping* went off inside him. Although, to be honest, probably more from empathy than attraction. Because she was right—he wasn't healed. Not by a long shot. Not when he'd still occasionally wake up in the middle of the night, his gut clenching when he realized he'd reached for someone who wasn't there. When he'd look into his son's eyes and see his own grief and anger mirrored there.

Emotions not dissimilar to what he'd just heard in Blythe's voice, it now occurred to him. To have Kym taken—no, *stolen*—from them… Wes hadn't known a person could feel that much pain and still function. But to a child, would a parent's abandonment hurt any less? Or be "gotten over" any more quickly?

"Do you know if that website still exists?" he asked, earning him a sharp frown.

"Uh, yeah. In fact, I'm one of the moderators. But—"

"Do you think it would help Jack?"

The frown didn't budge. "That's not for me to say, Wes."

He crossed his arms. "You moderate it, but you wouldn't recommend it."

A slight smile cracked the tension. "Obviously I think it's a great place. Since it saved my butt and all. But I was in my mid-teens. I'm not sure it's right for an eleven-year-old."

"Fair enough. But I'd still like to check it out."

A laughing couple walked by, diverting Blythe's attention for a moment. Then, on yet another sigh, she dug in her purse for a notepad, wrote something, tore off the paper and handed it to Wes.

He stared at the address for a moment, then looked at Blythe, caught the compassion in her eyes. For his kid, he assumed. Even so, he suddenly wanted to grab her by the shoulders and say, *Do you have any idea how great you are?* "What's your moderator name?"

The corners of her mouth lifted. "Like I'm going to tell you?"

"You don't play fair."

She gave him a quizzical look, then said, "I hear the kids are off next week for spring break, so I'll call Jack, set up a time when we can get together to start his room. Deal?"

"Sounds good to me," Wes said, wondering if she realized the kids' break coincided with his. Not that he'd be in residence full time—his campaign manager was already on his case about getting things rolling for reelection—but he would be around. For Jack's sake, if nothing else. And right now, as Wes watched Blythe walk off, her bright purple umbrella snapping open as a light drizzle began to fall, he found himself wondering…if things were different…if she…if he…

Sighing heavily, he flagged down a taxi, refusing to let the loneliness choke him.

As it happened, most of Blythe's other clients had kids off the next week as well, meaning they'd gone to wherever the well-to-do went for spring break. As a kid, she'd been lucky to get packed off to Nana's. Although since her cousins' vacations rarely jibed with hers she was usually left to her own devices, the same as she would have been in the Maryland suburb where she'd grown up. At least in St. Mary's there'd been the beach. And the boardwalk, with its shops and food stands, then as now the air spiked with the scents of grilled hot dogs and fried clams, a hundred different sunscreens, the ever-present tang of the bay. On which she now walked with Jack and Quinn, slurping down soft-serve ice cream cones and plotting out the Great Redesign project as the sun beat down on their heads and arms and backs.

The day was weirdly warm for April, enough to bring out shorts and sundresses, showcasing winter-pale legs and freshly varnished toes in flip-flops. Across the estuary, humidity smudged the demarcation between sky and water into a colorless blur. Even the gulls were lethargic, only a few with enough oomph to see if there was anything worth getting excited about. A few hardy souls, though, skirmished over a piece of soft pretzel somebody had dropped, squabbling like toddlers until a golden retriever rushed them, barking, gobbling up the pretzel when they flew away.

"So have you decided what you want to put in the room?" Blythe asked, taking a napkin to a glob of chocolate ice cream that had found its way to her white capris. Of course.

"Actually," Jack said, sucking a dribble of ice cream off his wrist, "now that it's empty? I'm thinking of keeping it like that."

Quinn gave him a horrified look, Hermione Granger to Jack's Ron Weasley. "Even though the walls look like they're diseased?"

Blythe chuckled. It was true, that wallpaper border had not given up without a fight. And by the time they patched up all the holes, the space did have a certain leprous vibe going on. "If you want to leave it, we certainly can," she said, not missing Quinn's you-have-*got*-to-be-kidding-me look. "But the sleeping bag on the hard floor will get old after a while."

"Yeah, I guess." Jack stuffed half the cone in his mouth, swirled it around, then popped it back out, not caring that ice cream now sheened half his chin. Blythe dug in her giant tote bag for another napkin, handing it over. Kid took the hint. "But I like sleeping on the floor. How about a mattress instead of a whole bed?"

"Don't see why not," Blythe said, shoving the rest of her own cone into her mouth, wondering why that last bite was always like a burst of happiness on her tongue. She'd grilled her younger cousin about Jack's behavior during the past week, but Quinn seemed to think the crisis had passed. Or at least had abated while his dad was home. Blythe took that to mean she'd been let off the hook as far as, well, whatever "everyone" expected her to do. And thank God for that. Since, as badly as she felt for the kid— for any kid in that much pain—there was a big difference between her anonymous work on the website and knowing what to actually say in real life.

Hey—she'd given Wes a heads-up about her and Quinn's

concerns, and that she could be a friend to Jack, if he was cool with that. But while, for Jack's sake, she'd felt impelled to come clean with his father about her "lost" years, she kept her work on the website, which not even her cousins knew about, a secret for a reason. Maybe she'd conquered her past, but it was still a dark period of her life she'd just as soon forget. And frankly, it wasn't anyone's business but hers. And Wes's, now—

Whoa. Hottie, dead ahead, ambling toward them in an Orioles ball cap and khaki shorts displaying muscled calves, a slightly wrinkled white polo showing off equally ripped forearms, and dimples just a'twinkin' away underneath a pair of badass sunglasses—

"Dad! You're back!"

"Hey, guy," Wes said, swinging one of those forearms around his son's shoulders and that smile in Blythe's direction, and she sent up a short prayer that ice cream wasn't dribbled all over her chin. Or chest. Not that she was holding out much hope for either. "Meeting ended early, Grandma said all of you were down here. So what's up?"

"Still trying to decide on the room," Blythe said, pretending to blow her nose in one of the napkins in order to clandestinely wipe her chin. Although there wasn't a darn thing she could do about the splotch on her pants.

"Got paint yet?"

"Next on the list, actually."

"Good," Wes said, holding her gaze. Or so she assumed. Hard to tell through the Ray-Bans. "Because I've cleared the calendar for the next couple of days to help." He slid his fingers into his shorts' pockets, the wind plastering the polo to his pecs, and all manner of things Blythe had willed to shut up and go to sleep woke up with a start.

Gasping.

"Then, well…let's go choose some paint," she said.

Whether or not Wes had checked out the website or mentioned it to Jack, she mused as they trooped out to the parking lot and her car, she had no idea. Nor was that the point. The point was getting Jack over this hump. And from what she'd been able to tell since they'd been back in St. Mary's, the man was trying. She had to give him that. Yes, he still had business to tend to that didn't include Jack—the same as any working parent—but when he was home, he was *there*. And watching him try…well.

Flutters, she had them. Unwelcome though they might be.

When they got to her car, the kids piled into the back and Wes got into the passenger seat up front before anyone could discuss seating arrangements, so Blythe decided to play along like this was all perfectly okay before the weird feeling in the pit of her tum-tum found its way to her face. Not exactly panic, but close. Because, ohmygoodness, didn't they look like the perfect young family, traipsing into the Home Depot, the kids yammering at each other and Wes touching her elbow to steer her toward the paint section. Like, you know, she might somehow miss the ginormous PAINT sign overhead.

Then—*then*—he stood close enough as they riffled through the blue and green paint chips to encroach on her personal space, which her poor little brain had no idea what to do with. Especially the part that processed scents, sending them either to the "ewww" or "mmmm" receptors in said brain. Because right now, those receptors were "mmming" their little hearts out.

"How about this?" Wes said, holding up a blue paint chip to his son that was a tad on the bright side. Like, eyeball-spinning bright. No wonder he'd let his wife do all the decorating.

Jack made a face—thankfully—and held up a very nice

muted slate blue that Blythe might have chosen herself. Kid had taste. And had, also thankfully, given up on the idea of painting all four walls different colors. The palette was coming together—soft, underwater colors the boy said "made him feel good" with white and bright orange accents.

"Dad. Seriously?"

Frowning, Wes looked at the swatch again. Through, Blythe realized, his sunglasses, which he hadn't removed. Clearly puzzled, he glanced up again. "What's wrong with it?"

Chuckling, Blythe tugged off the glasses, belatedly realizing how intimate the gesture was. Especially when Wes's eyes met hers and...

Dropped right back to the swatch. "Oh. Wow. Yeah, buddy, I see your point. This one—" he nodded at Jack's pick "—is much better. Much more like something your mother would have chosen."

"That's what I thought, too," the boy said, sliding his gaze to Blythe, and she thought, *Got it.*

Yeah, she needed to remember that nobody here was interested in wedging a new person into their lives. Wes and Jack, because their hearts were still sore. And her, because she had way too much self-respect to go that route again.

Flutters be damned.

"Here," Blythe said, handing Wes his glasses, her smile a little crispy around the edges before she said to Jack, "Good choice. Go tell the guy at the paint counter we need three gallons of satin finish, then meet us over there—" she pointed "—for brushes and rollers and stuff."

Jack and his trusty sidekick took off for the mixing counter as Blythe yanked the cart around and started smartly toward the painting supply aisle. Wes considered taking the cart from her, then decided she looked like a woman who definitely needed something to hang on to right now. "It almost sounds as if you're going to do the painting yourself."

"With Jack's help, yeah. I am." Not looking at him, she snatched up a package of rollers, tossed them into the cart. Wes noticed her cheeks were a mite on the pink side.

"I assume that's not your usual modus operandi."

An edging tool, roll of blue masking tape and three cutting brushes followed. "Nope."

"Then why—"

"Because this isn't only about changing Jack's room, it's about…" Finally, she met his gaze again, the smile a little less brittle. Even though caution filmed her eyes. A reaction to that funny business with the glasses, he guessed. Although truth be told he hadn't found it all that funny. Pathetic, is more the word he'd use, considering his sucker-punched reaction to the easy familiarity. How, for that breath of a moment, he'd wanted…

He'd wanted his old life back. Wanted, he thought with a savage stab to his chest, Kym back, wanted the teasing and the laughter and that deep-seated peace that comes from knowing someone else had your back. Always. Except that wasn't possible, and indulging such musings was not only pointless, but would only keep both him and his son mired in grief. In the past.

"It's about helping Jack move forward," Blythe said, as if reading his mind. Although the caution was still there, it seemed to have stepped to one side enough to let compassion take center stage. "You wanted my help, this is how I decided I can best give it. Not by talking, but by doing. And I think Jack will feel more connected to the room if he's part of the process. More connected to…"

"What?"

"The present," she said, then added two drop cloths and a couple of roller pans to the growing pile.

Wes hadn't been on the website five minutes before he realized it wasn't really geared to kids as young as Jack. But even if it had been, he and his son needed to work through this together. In person. Because as Blythe had pointed out, at least he and Jack did have each other.

And Wes was determined not to let his son forget that.

"How did you get him to change his mind? About wanting to keep everything the same in his room?"

"I didn't. And I never do." Her mouth canted, the smile more relaxed this time. "I just plant the seeds. Then back off and let them germinate." Her shoulders—bare, pale, a little bony, truth be told—bumped. "But the worst thing a designer can do is impose his or her own ideas on a client. Because, ultimately, if the end result doesn't feel like them, they'll hate it in a few months. And blame you for it. But..." A groove dug into the space between her brows. "But it just seems to me," she said gently, "Jack needs to feel in control. Responsible for his own decisions." Those astute blue eyes grazed his. "But with the support and guidance to make the right ones. Which I never had."

Oddly, they were the only ones in the aisle. And, yes, Wes took advantage of that, crossing his arms and holding her gaze captive. "We're not talking about paint colors anymore, are we?"

Blythe laughed, a low, chesty sound Wes found extremely...appealing. And a trifle on the melancholy side, though she probably didn't realize it.

"I'm sorry. I'm..." She bit her lip.

"Going to finish that thought."

She lightly rapped her knuckles on the cart handle, then sighed.

"When my father left, and my mother withdrew, I felt

like a dog who'd been dumped in the woods. Abandoned to fend for myself. Emotionally, anyway—I was never in danger of starving, even if dinner consisted of frozen pizza more often than not. But it was as if my mother didn't have the resources or stamina to deal with her own heartbreak— or regrets, whatever—and mine, too." Another shoulder bump. "Hence my drift to the dark side."

"What about your grandmother? Your cousins?"

"Nana wasn't much better, off in her own world. And my cousins…they were kids, too. Not that I didn't feed off them—heck, now that I look back, we fed off each other—but…"

Turning away, she gave the cart a shove, pushing it down the still-vacant aisle. Wes followed, grabbing the gallon of white semigloss paint off the shelf when she went for it. His bare forearm grazed her shoulder, cool and smooth, and longing spurted through him. But not, he realized, for what had been, but for what could be. A future, he thought that was called. Because suddenly the thought of spending the rest of what he hoped would be a long life alone was not sitting well.

Setting the paint in the cart, he noticed Blythe leaning heavily on the cart's handle, her forehead slightly creased as she regarded its contents.

"But…?"

She straightened, then let out another rough laugh. "I'm not being overly dramatic when I say that it's a miracle I survived at all. Guess I'm made of sterner stuff than I realized. And I also guess my experiences made me who I am, so I can't completely regret them. However…" Her eyes shifted to take in the kids, staggering toward them, laughing, the paint cans dangling from their hands. "There are times when I wonder, if I'd had the kind of support Jack has, in you and your parents—"

She shook her head, then started to steer the cart toward the kids. Wes grabbed the side, stopping her, getting a puzzled look for his efforts.

"That you'd be different?"

The gaze that tangled with his was completely devoid of self-pity. But not, he didn't think, of pain. Scabbed over though it may have been. "Yes."

He glanced over, gauged how long he had before the kids reached them. "Look, I'm sorry for what you went through," he said quietly. Hurriedly. "I truly am. No kid should have to deal with that. But as you said, your experiences made you who you are now. And that person, from everything I can tell, is pretty damn amazing."

She was still gawking at him like he'd sprouted an extra head when the kids clumsily hefted the paint cans into the cart.

Chapter Six

Dad's laugh made Jack whip his head around, then jump when he spattered white paint all over his shirt. He muttered a bad word, trying to wipe off the paint with his wrist, but it was too late.

"What's wrong?" Quinn said, sitting a few feet away, painting her own section of baseboard. She'd pulled her hair into this ponytail or something, making her look like she had curly orange seaweed growing out of her head.

"Got paint on myself. Hand me that rag."

"Please."

"Please. Jeez."

She tossed it over, then shook her head, making the seaweed-hair jiggle. Sometimes he wondered if it was weird—if *he* was weird—because his best friend was a girl. Then again, Quinn liked playing video games and football and skateboarding, even though she wasn't very good at it. In other words, not a normal girl. Except then she said, "Blythe told you to put on something you didn't care about," *exactly* like a girl, and Jack glared at her skinny back. He dumped the rag, not sure what was bugging him more—that she was right, that he'd ruined his favorite shirt or that Dad was laughing again.

At Blythe.

Jack dipped his brush into the paint pan, sneaking a look across the room at her. She'd changed into a pair of messy overalls over a sleeveless shirt, and her hair stuck up all over her head—it had blue paint in it, too, in places. She wasn't even pretty, really. Not like Mom. So why Dad would even like her—like *that,* he meant—it didn't make sense. But he obviously did.

And that ticked Jack off. Not that he didn't like Blythe okay—actually, before this, he'd liked her a lot—but…so, finally he gets a chance to spend some time with Dad, only there's Blythe, too. Yeah, she was the designer and all, but really—it wasn't like he and Dad couldn't't've painted the room themselves, right?

"Okie-doke," Dad said, grinning, as he wiped his hands on another rag. He was almost as messy as Jack was. And goofy happy, which made Jack's stomach hurt. "Anybody up for hamburgers tonight?"

Jack frowned. "Really?" He could barely remember the last time his dad had grilled. Not since Mom had died, for sure. But then, he got elected to Congress right after that, so it wasn't like he'd had a lot of time for hanging out in his own backyard and cooking hamburgers.

"Really," Dad said. "Your grandmother said she bought ground beef and all the fixings. And heaven knows it's warm enough. So what do you say?" Then he turned the grin on Blythe. A grin than made Jack feel like punching something. "What do you say?"

Looking a little surprised, actually, she glanced at Jack before looking at Dad again. "I'm invited?"

"Of course. Quinn, too, if she wants."

"Actually," Quinn said, getting to her feet and brushing off her butt, even though somehow she wasn't dirty, "Ryder said we're going over to the inn tonight for dinner. So I can't. In fact—" She looked at her watch, which she'd gotten last week for her eleventh birthday. Mickey Mouse. Dumb. "—I'm supposed to meet him there in a few minutes, so I need to go, anyway." Her eyes met Jack's, all conflicted, like she knew she was abandoning him. "Sorry."

"You need me to drive you, sweetie?" Blythe said, swiping her hand across her cheek and leaving another blue smear. Blythe was always calling everybody *sweetie.* Annoying.

"It's five houses away, I think I can manage," Quinn said with an eye roll, then waved to everyone and disappeared. It was everything Jack could do not to run after her, beg to come along. But that would be lame.

"I'll go make myself presentable and then get the grill going," Dad said, then looked at Blythe. "Unless you need me to help clean up here—"

"Nope, got it. And, uh, thanks for the invitation."

"No problem," Dad said, then left the room.

"You done with that brush?" Blythe asked, banging the lid back on the blue paint can with a hammer.

"Almost," Jack said, staring hard at the baseboard, hating that his eyes were burning.

Hating that Mom was gone and never coming back, hating that Dad was acting like helping to paint his room was going to make up for him leaving again at the end of the week. Hating the way he looked at Blythe. Not exactly like he used to look at Mom, but close enough.

Bang. Bang. Bang.

Yeah. Like that, he thought, his eyes sliding to Blythe.

Didn't take a rocket scientist—or a child psychologist—to figure out that Jack was pissed about her being there. Any more than it took one to figure out that his dad sorta-kinda had a crush on her. Of course, Blythe sortakinda had a crush on Wes, too—heh—but she could handle it. She wasn't so sure Wes could, what with grief still short-circuiting his receptors and all.

And for damn sure she knew Jack couldn't.

Blythe gathered up the rollers and brushes, dumping them into the nearly empty roller pan to take outside and wash, all the while contemplating her own stupidity. Had she really thought all it would take to fix the kid was to involve him in his room remodel?

Worse, had she been so naive as to think that having his father help them would fix things faster? And better? Sure, the boy missed his dad, and boom, there was Dad, helping to paint the boy's room. On paper, a slam dunk. In reality…

Big sigh time. Because she'd totally discounted the possibility that she and Wes might get along a little *too* well, and that Jack would pick up on that, twist it six ways to Sunday and spit it right back in their faces. Hers, anyway. Somehow she had the feeling Wes hadn't figured that out yet.

"I don't have to stay, you know."

Sure enough, narrowed eyes cut right to hers. What she could see under the boy band bangs, that is.

"Huh?"

"For dinner. If it makes you uncomfortable, I don't have to stay."

Frowning hard, Jack turned away again, like he was

going to finish up painting that baseboard if it took him the rest of spring break. "But Dad invited you."

"True. Doesn't mean I can't come up with some reason to back out."

Another glance, before he skootched on his butt to reach the next section of baseboard. "Dad likes you."

And there it was. "I like your father, too. He's a nice man." She took a damp rag to a splotch on the floor. "But there's nothing going on between us."

"Like I care if there is."

"Of course you care, sweetie," she said, watching his back go rigid. "As well you should. But I can assure you that right now, this—" she swept out one arm, indicating the room "—is about *you*. And the last thing I want is for you to think I'm coming between you and your dad. Because I'm not. And I have no intention of doing that. Ever."

Again, his head swung to hers. But this time his gaze held. "You mean that?"

You have no idea, how much I mean that. "Absolutely."

The boy seemed to consider this for a few seconds, then got up to toss the brush into the pan, looking around the room with his hands jammed in his pockets. "I remember when Mom painted this room. Sort of." He paused. "I was pretty little."

"Your mom did a great job with the house," Blythe said carefully. "She was very talented—"

"It's not *fair*," Jack blurted out, banging his hand into a just-painted blue wall, leaving a white smudge. Then he turned to her, anger flashing in wet eyes. The eyes of a child still too young to cope with such a horrible loss. Blythe's own eyes stung in empathy, remembering her own anger and confusion, so many years ago.

"No, it's not," she said simply, surprised the boy was still there, still talking to her, especially considering his obvious antipathy toward her. Or at least, his antipathy toward his father's interest in her. "I felt exactly the same way when my dad left."

For the moment, however, curiosity apparently edged out the anger. "Left? Like, on a trip or something?"

"No. Left me and my mother. For good."

The boy's pale brows crashed over his nose. "How old were you?"

"A little older than you are now. Still a kid, though. I never heard from him again."

"Like, not at all?"

"Not even for my birthday. Nothing. As if he simply forgot I existed."

"Wow."

"Yeah. I keep thinking I should try to look him up, see if I could find him. And then I think...why?"

The boy smirked. "How about so you could tell him what a loser he is?"

She blew a laugh through her nose. "Now *that's* a tempting idea."

"But at least he's still alive, right?" Jack said. Blythe flinched. *Idiot.*

"I don't know, actually. But I think my mom would have heard if he'd died. And she's never said anything, so..." She shrugged, then picked up the pan with the dirty brushes and rollers. "Better get these cleaned up before the paint dries on them. Um...wanna help?"

Jack seemed to consider this for a moment, then nodded. Even took the pan from her before they tromped downstairs and outside, where she squatted to wash everything in the icy water from the backyard faucet, the breeze off the inlet at the back of the property instantly freezing her hands despite the sun slanting across her back. Jack stood, watching her, his own hands rammed in his pockets as the paint-stained water ran in rivulets through the new grass.

"I'm sorry about your dad." Doggedly massaging paint out of a waterlogged roller, Blythe looked up, barely able to make out the boy's features with the sun behind him. "Seriously," he said, "that sucks. But that doesn't mean…" Flat-mouthed, he looked away.

Her chest cramping, Blythe thought of Mel, who still couldn't speak about her dad, who'd died suddenly when she was sixteen, without tearing up. Of the gut-wrenching posts from some of the kids on the website, who'd lost parents to illness, accident, combat—leaving vast, yawning chasms in their hearts.

Sure, she ached for Jack the way she ached for those kids. More, because she did know him personally. Even so, she'd never had her father's love, so she truthfully couldn't say she'd lost much when he left. Except for, perhaps, that seesaw of hope and disappointment that had defined her childhood. But to lose not only the person you loved but the love itself…

"I know, sweetie," she said. "I really do." She suddenly realized a certain sidekick was missing. "Where's Bear?"

"Probably in the kitchen with Grandma. Because, as Mom used to say, where there's food, there's hope."

Blythe laughed. After a moment, Jack hunkered down beside her to scrub one of the brushes in the running water.

"It's cold," she said.

"I don't mind." A rainbow flashed in the sun when he flicked the brush off to the side. "I also don't mind if you stay for dinner."

"You sure?"

"No."

Another few seconds passed, filled with the sounds of robin trills and splashing water, the faint calls of gulls. "I think your mom would be very proud of you," Blythe finally said, glancing over in time to catch the boy's slight smile.

Dinner done, Wes's parents had retreated inside to watch TV, and Blythe had excused herself to, Wes assumed, "powder her nose," as his grandmother used to say. Jack was down in the yard, close to the water, playing catch with Bear. Who probably needed to run off all those hamburger scraps Blythe had kept feeding him all evening, declaring she was a total sucker for the dog's pitiful expression.

As he scraped the grill, Wes watched boy and dog, smiling at Jack's laughter and wondering what had transpired between Blythe and Jack to blunt the irritation he'd seen in his son's eyes when, without thinking, Wes invited Blythe to dinner. Because his already touchy son probably assumed Wes saw Blythe as a substitute for Jack's mother.

Which, of course, was absurd, if for no other reason than there'd never be a substitute for Kym. A fact Wes needed to make clear before Jack blew things out of proportion.

And before Wes even had the chance to see...well, if there *was* a chance.

Yes, Blythe had baggage—baggage Wes had no idea if he could even shift, let alone help her get rid of. But she also had what some people might call soul. And a strength of spirit that had clearly seen her through what must have been a pretty lousy childhood. Or at least a disappointing one. That, after everything she'd been through, she could care about others as much as she obviously did stirred something inside Wes, the likes of which he hadn't felt in a long, long time.

Something strong enough, he realized as he watched Jack throw a ball to Bear, to possibly shift his own baggage.

And that stirring, in turn, turned up a kind of hope—that if he was willing to take a peek around his own pile, what was to say she wasn't, as well?

Hey. Weirder things happened. Like getting elected when he'd been polling ten points behind his opponent. Still, Jack was his first priority. As carefully as Wes knew he needed to tread with Blythe, that was nothing compared with how he had to handle Jack. Something he wanted badly enough to pray for it…which he hadn't done since Kym's death, when he'd pretty much figured God didn't give a damn about him. About any of them.

Now, though, as he carried the grill off the deck and down into the cool, damp grass to wash it off, he thought maybe—

"Hey, beast!" he said, laughing, when Bear poked the slimy ball into the center of Wes's back. The grill abandoned, Wes twisted around to grab the ball still clamped in Bear's teeth, indulging the game of tug-of-war until the dog released it, backing up and barking, dashing after the ball when Wes slung it far out into the yard.

Maybe, sometimes, it was just about letting go. Trusting. That, in this case, Blythe Broussard had landed in their lives for a reason. And that the smartest thing Wes could do was keep his mouth shut and let things shake out the way they were supposed to.

And then know that everyone involved would be blessed.

One way or another.

Rubbing the hand lotion she'd found on the half bath's sink into her paint-ravaged hands, Blythe wandered back onto the deck in time to see Wes, Jack and the dog playing some sort of bizarre three-way catch in the sunset's last hurrah. As far as she could tell, the dog was winning. In fact, Bear took off with the ball in his jowls, sending both

Wes and Jack scrambling after him from opposite directions, colliding in a jumble of bare calves and black fur and laughter. A moment later, Wes sat up, grinning like a goon, the ball held aloft…but only until Jack snatched it from him a moment later.

She laughed, the sound apparently reaching Wes on the same breeze that toyed with her already crazed hair, soothing skin she hadn't realized was heated. Which heated more when a panting, grinning, messy-haired Wes glanced over. Oh, my.

"Come join us," he yelled, raking a hand through that hair. Flashing those damn dimples. "You can be on the dog's team."

I can't, she wanted to say. Needed to say.

I can't, because I have to get back home, to my safe, solitary little life, the one where there's no dimpled, sexy, stalwart man tugging at my heart and his young, needy son tugging even harder.

Except then—speaking of tugging—as if someone or something had taken her by the hand, she found herself down the steps and out in the yard, now playing some strange little game of catch/fetch, the rules of which Wes seemed to be making up on the fly. Although mostly it was about chasing the dog every time he got the ball, which was roughly every thirty seconds. And yes, Blythe felt like the kid she'd never really been, laughing and running around like a lunatic and sliding in the grass, slippery from an earlier rain.

At one point, though, a cramp in her side forced her to stop. Bending over to wait out the cramp and catch her breath, she watched father and son continue their game, and she was struck by what she could only call the expression of release on their faces. As though all it had taken to break grief's hold had been a few minutes of silliness, of chasing a dumb dog around their backyard.

And at that moment, as the stitch subsided and she straightened up, smiling as she witnessed their precarious connection solidify before her eyes, she also realized how hard she was falling for both of them. A thought that produced a cramp of another kind, one that seized her heart.

Because it was only right that Wes cement his relationship with his son, that they both find their way back to happiness, and each other, after the tragedy that had shaken both of them so badly. With Wes's career that wouldn't be easy, although Blythe felt certain if anyone could pull off this particular juggling act it would be Wes. But the thing was, she'd finally realized there was no shame in wanting to be first in someone's life. Or at least share the podium. To constantly feel she had to beg for scraps, however...

Briefly, she considered stealing away before anyone noticed. But that would be rude. If not cowardly. And anyway, another couple of days, max, and Jack's room would be done and that would be that. Right?

"Look sharp!" Wes called, tossing the ball in her direction, barely giving her time to hike up those big girl panties before lunging for it with everything she had.

Or at least as much as it seemed wise to give.

"Jack!" Wes's mother called from the back deck. "Come help me for a minute, would you?"

His son tromped off. But with a pointed look over his shoulder at Blythe, halfheartedly toasting a marshmallow in the fire pit Wes had dug five or six summers ago, her pensive expression a warning sign if ever there was one.

And yet, Wes didn't want the evening to end. How long had it been since he'd felt like that? Even if he sincerely doubted Blythe felt the same way. Yes, she was still here, but the set to her jaw, the crease between her eyebrows, pretty much negated the "Aren't we all having fun here?" smile she'd pasted on after dinner.

The thing was, her smiles and laughter before then— he'd bet his life those had been genuine enough. So what the hell had happened?

And why?

Leaning back in a weather-worn Adirondack chair, a lukewarm can of Dr. Pepper propped on the arm, Wes gave his curiosity enough leash to probably hang himself.

"Everything okay?" he said, tilting the can to his lips, and her eyes zinged to his.

But only for a moment. She pulled her marshmallow out of the fire, blowing on the charred lump for a few seconds before pinching it off the stick, its melted guts stretching and sagging for several inches before she stuffed it into her mouth. "I haven't done this since I was a kid," she said as she chewed, then dug for another marshmallow from the open bag by her feet, impaling it on the stick and consigning it to its fiery doom. "Heaven."

Wes propped his elbow on the chair arm, his cheek planted on his fist. "You didn't answer my question."

"Well aware of that," she said, carefully turning the stick. "Not going to, either."

Chuckling, Wes hunched forward, knees apart as he rolled the soda can between his palms. "I suppose that's better than lying. If barely."

With a spectacular *whumph,* her marshmallow ignited. On a muttered "Damn," Blythe jerked it to safety, dousing the flames with a single breath. "I was going to leave earlier. When we were still playing ball with the dog."

"Why?"

She plucked the blackened sugar shell off the melted center, squishing it between her fingers before devouring it. She chewed for a moment, then swallowed. "Because I didn't want to interfere with what was happening between you and Jack."

"Then why'd you stay?"

The corners of her mouth curved. Barely. "Because it's been about a million years since I just...played. And," she said, stabbing another marshmallow, "having no idea when such an opportunity might come along again, it seemed silly to pass it up."

His eyes on the marshmallow, Wes said softly, "It's feels almost that long since I played, too."

"I can imagine."

Dangling the can between his knees, he watched the flames dance. "I remember as a kid being so impatient for childhood to be over. So I could do all the grown-up things that looked so cool. Now I wonder what I was thinking."

This time, Blythe removed the marshmallow before the fire incinerated it. Plucked it off, popped it into her mouth.

"You know," Wes said, "we have chocolate and graham crackers, too."

"I know." She nibbled goo off her fingers. "But why dilute the good stuff?" When Wes chuckled again, her eyes slid to his for a moment before she slumped forward, poking her empty stick into the ashes at the fire's edge. "I know what you mean, about being impatient to grow up." Listlessly, she prodded one ember until it exploded into a tiny shower of sparks. "But God knows I don't miss my childhood. Even if I sometimes think I wouldn't mind a redo."

Aching for her, Wes sagged back into the chair again. "You're going to make a terrific mom someday."

She let out a harsh laugh. "Did you not hear what I said before—?"

"You love kids, Blythe. And you're great with them."

Another ember softly exploded. "Doesn't mean I want the full-time responsibility."

"I don't believe you." When her eyes swung to his, he shrugged. "I mean it. Not in the long term."

She stopped torturing the stick, tossing it instead into the grass beside her. "Then let me put it this way—this self-confidence thing I have going? It's all an act. Because inside I'm about as solid as…as a melted marshmallow. That doesn't exactly make me an ideal candidate for motherhood." Her gaze once more touched his. "Among other things, I'm pretty broken."

"You really think that?"

She let out a quiet laugh then said, "I *know* it. I may seem to have it all together, but trust me—it's all duct tape and mirrors." A breath left her lungs. "I'm an illusion of my own creating, Wes. And you and Jack—you both deserve better than that."

"In other words…you're warning me off."

Her shoulders hitched. "I'm not immune to picking up on things. Or to feeling them. So a heads-up seemed prudent."

"And if I don't heed your warning?"

"You don't have a choice. Look," she said quietly when he snorted, "you have no idea how badly my ego would like to run with this. I've never met anyone like you, and I'm not going to deny the chemistry here. Not to mention that I *like* you. And I'm already fond of Jack. More fond than I should be, given the circumstances. But I do know myself, at least well enough to know that your life…" She shook her head. "It would never be a good fit."

He frowned. "Because of my career?"

"Partly, yes. I've… I…" Clearing her throat, she looked back at the fire. "I'd be a millstone around your neck, Wes. For many reasons. Not the least of which is my background.

But more than that…being in a relationship is like a drug for me. One I far too easily become dependent on. And God knows I've had enough psychology courses to understand why, that I'm still looking for someone to give me what my parents didn't. And as long as I'm tempted to look outside myself instead of *within* myself…" Her head wagged.

"So what you're saying is," Wes said, irritated far more than he had any right to be, "you're going to keep everyone who might want inside *with* you at arm's length?"

"That's the plan, yep."

"And that's the biggest crock I think I've ever heard." He smashed the now-empty can into the chair's arm. "And trust me, I've heard some doozies."

Finally she rose, dusting flecks of burned marshmallow off her overalls. "Would you rather I had run away? Run from the truth?"

"Just because you stayed doesn't mean you're not running."

Her gaze swerved to his. And he suspected her flushed cheeks weren't due solely to the firelight. "Oh, come on, Wes—we're both hurting. So is Jack. Nobody's in any position to form new attachments at this point—"

"And did it ever occur to you," he said, shoving himself to his feet, "that maybe the only way any of us could move past the pain *is* to form new attachments? To move forward instead of cowering in some corner of the past?"

His vehemence took him as much by surprise as it obviously did Blythe.

"Wes…you're not listening—"

"To which part? When you said we were all hurting? Not going to argue with you there. I mean, you obviously are. And, yes, I miss my wife, who was also my best friend for more than half my life. A friend who I know would bean me if she thought for one moment I was wallowing in my misery. Or her memory."

Taking advantage of Blythe's apparent paralysis, he stepped closer. "Or the part where you tossed your childhood indiscretions in my path, as if I'd give a damn about any of that? Or maybe you mean the part about your being afraid of letting anyone get too close?"

Her eyes bugged. "I d-didn't say that."

"The hell you didn't." Wes rammed his hands in his shorts' pockets, lowering his voice when he noticed Jack and the dog coming back out onto the deck. "So, yeah, I heard. And you know what? I'm not buying it. Any of it. Because let me tell you something—you can't keep endlessly giving without accepting, too. One doesn't really work without the other. Not well, at any rate." He stepped closer and whispered. "Fear's a bitch. And trust me, nobody knows that better than I do."

For two, three seconds their gazes held, until Jack and Bear roared down the deck stairs and over to them. Then, as if startled out of a trance, Blythe stormed across the lawn and around the side of the house, not even bothering to say goodbye.

Jack watched Blythe take off, feeling like somebody'd tied his insides in knots. Or his brain. Or both. Especially when he caught the look on Dad's face as he watched Blythe go. He hadn't been able to hear what they were saying, but it sure looked like they were having a fight. Or at least "words," as Grandma would say. She and Grandpa had "words" a lot, but since nobody stayed mad for very long, Jack had finally stopped worrying about it.

It was funny, but before his grandparents came to live with Dad and him, Jack never understood how you could get mad at somebody you liked. Now that he was older, though, he got it. Sort of. After all, he and Quinn made each other mad all the time, and they were still friends. Sometimes people just didn't agree, no matter how well they got along.

Of course, sometimes people were idiots and said stupid stuff, but somehow he didn't think that was what was going on here. Between Blythe and his dad, he meant. Because he was also beginning to realize that, actually, the more people liked each other, the more they did fight. Had words, whatever. Not that he'd ever heard Mom and Dad argue, but for all he knew they had, only he'd never heard them.

And at this rate his brain was going to melt and drip right out of his ears.

"Why'd Blythe leave?" he asked when he got close enough for Dad to hear him.

"She was tired," Dad said, stooping to pat Bear, who'd flopped down at his feet. "And she wants to get an early start on your room tomorrow. Want some s'mores?" He shifted to snatch the marshmallow bag off the ground. "There's still enough heat in the fire—"

"Why were you fighting?"

Frowning, Dad looked up. "We weren't—"

"Sure sounded like it."

Dad handed him a stick and the bag, then sat on the wooden bench across from the two chairs. "I suppose it did," he said, then sighed. "She said some things that I guess pushed me over the edge. Not because of what she said, but why she said it."

"Huh?"

He waved Jack over, took the stick and bag from him and jabbed a marshmallow on the point, handed it back. Like Jack couldn't do that himself, honestly. "I can't go into details, partly because I don't know them all and partly because it wouldn't be right to do that without Blythe's permission. But I gather there've been a lot of people in Blythe's life who didn't treat her very well. Who didn't love her the way she should have been loved. And because of that, she's…leery of letting people get too close."

"What's that mean?"

"Leery?"

"Yeah."

"Afraid."

Lowering his marshmallow toward the fire, Jack felt his forehead tighten. Blythe sure didn't act like she was afraid. Of anything. But then, neither did Jack, not if he could help it. Even though the truth was he sometimes felt so scared, so alone—even when other people were around—he felt like his chest was going to cave in.

"But…she's so nice."

Well, she was. Maybe Jack didn't want her to come between him and Dad, but that didn't mean she was a bad person or anything.

His father gave him a funny look, then smiled. Sort of. "Which is exactly why I got mad." When Jack frowned harder, Dad said, "Because it chaps my hide when I see good people cut themselves off from…from living a full life because they believe they don't deserve it. Or they're scared."

The marshmallow went up in flames; Dad grabbed for the stick like Jack was some baby, even though he'd already jerked it toward him to blow out the fire. "So you like Blythe, huh?" Jack asked, deciding against telling his father he'd asked Blythe the same question about him. But it wouldn't hurt to know what was going on. Where he stood.

The dog jumped up, barking at nothing. Dad watched him for a moment, then said, "Why wouldn't I like her? As you said, she's a nice lady—"

"And I'm not a little kid, okay?"

Dad didn't say anything for a long time, which made the knots get tighter inside Jack's stomach. Then his father clamped the back of his neck, rubbing it for a moment before letting it slap back on the bench's arm. "And I need to remember that. You want the truth? Yes, I like her. In exactly the boy-girl way you mean. But there's a very long road between thinking 'This is someone I'd like to know better' and thinking of her like—"

"Like you thought about Mom?"

Dad leaned forward, his elbows resting on his knees. "Does it scare you, to think that someday I might want to get married again?"

"Cripes, Dad! Mom just died!"

"It's been two years, Pup."

Jack nearly flinched—his father hadn't called him that in…God. Years. But if he thought that was going to change anything—

"You want to *marry* Blythe?"

"Let's back up a couple hundred steps, okay?" his father said with a short laugh. "What I said was, I like her. And I'd like to get to know her better. It's nothing I planned, or even thought about. Frankly, I'm pretty surprised, since, after your mother—"

"But she's nothing like Mom!"

"No, she's not. And you're determined not to let me finish what I was saying, aren't you? Come here," he said, patting the empty space on the bench beside him. Jack didn't want to go. But he did, too. And when he did, and Dad pulled him close the way he used to do when Jack was little, he had to admit it felt good. Not that he'd ever let anybody else see it, but whatever. "It really doesn't matter what I think," Dad said over Jack's head, "or how I feel, if Blythe's not open to the idea. And since she's made it very clear she's not…" Jack felt Dad shrug again. "There's no point fretting about something that's probably not going to happen."

"Probably?"

"Very probably." He paused, then said, "I can fix what *I* broke. Or at least give it my best shot. But I'm not sure I can fix what somebody else broke. Besides—" he gave Jack's shoulders a squeeze "—between you and my work... it's all moot."

"What's that mean?"

"Not worth thinking about."

But Jack could tell Dad was still thinking about it—about Blythe. Hard, too. Because that's how he was. In fact, now that Jack thought about it, his dad was all *about* fixing things, wasn't he? Stuff around the house, people's problems, whatever. In fact, hadn't Dad said that's why he'd run for Congress?

And now that Jack thought about it, maybe he was kind of like that, too. It's why he liked puzzles. Even the really hard ones. Slipping from underneath Dad's arm, he squatted in front of the fire, his arms wrapped tightly around his knees. Bear came up to him and slurped his cheek, almost knocking Jack on his butt before he ran off again, disappearing into the darkness, and Jack felt his forehead crunch as he looked out where the dog had gone.

No, this was definitely worth thinking about. Because no matter what Dad said, Jack knew he wouldn't let this thing with Blythe go until he'd figured it out. He also knew Mom had been Dad's only girlfriend, before they got married. So that he was even interested in Blythe...this was huge.

Dad's cell phone rang. Behind him, Jack heard his father answer, felt him touch Jack's shoulder before walking back toward the house. Work stuff, probably. Jack twisted partway around, watching, thinking if things did somehow work out between Dad and Blythe, he'd probably *never* see him.

A thought that made him want to throw up.

Chapter Seven

As a child, Blythe thought as she watched the delivery duo assemble the new platform bed/desk combo that had eventually won out over a mattress on the floor, she'd only truly felt safe when she was in control. Or at least believed she was. Until, eventually, it dawned on her that no matter what she did, good or bad, it didn't make a lick of difference. That the acting out hadn't been about being in control at all. Exactly the opposite, in fact. Because the harder she vied for attention, the more she'd actually ceded that control to someone else.

A lesson she didn't fully "get" until after her divorce, when she finally realized that being a good person and remaining single were not mutually exclusive concepts. That she could like people, even want to help them, without expecting anything in return. A philosophy she still believed to be true. And, for her, eminently workable. So why, pray, had that last conversation with Wes left her so shaken?

He wasn't around today, thank God. Neither was Jack, since Wes had taken the kid with him to Annapolis, both to chat up his constituency and to tour the Naval Academy. A deliberate move, apparently, since when she'd arrived that morning Wes's mother had expressed surprise at the sudden change in plans. So either the man was giving her space, or she'd finally pissed him off.

One could only hope.

"All done," the delivery guy said, his grin bright in a dark, slightly sweaty face. "That work for you where we put it? 'Cause we can shift it some if you want—"

"No, no…it's perfect. Here," she said, grabbing her purse and digging out twenties for the each of the two men. But the first one shook his head.

"We're not supposed to accept tips, ma'am—"

"You got kids?"

"Uh, yes, ma'am. We both do."

"Then use it to buy something for them, or take them to the movies or whatever."

After an exchanged glance, the guys grinned and took the money. "Then thank you. You have a nice day, now. And you have any problems, you call the store, ask for Elton, you hear?"

"I'll be sure to do that. Thanks again. It looks great."

The men lumbered off, leaving Blythe alone in the room. She'd opened the windows to let in the breeze off the inlet; a few more photographs to hang on what she'd dubbed the "gallery" wall, and she was done. She prayed Jack liked it. Or at least found some peace here.

"Oh…" His grandmother stood in the doorway, her hand pressed to her cheek. "Doesn't this look wonderful?"

"Thanks. Come take a look around."

Candace stepped inside, eyes alight. "It's perfect. In fact, it looks like something his mother would have done."

"I'll take that as a compliment," Blythe said, kicking aside the ridiculous ping of annoyance about someone she'd never met. And never would. Well, unless there really was an afterlife. Although considering the plethora of souls that had to be drifting around up there, or wherever, by now, what were the odds she'd run into that one? So not a big worry, that.

Then she started slightly when Wes's mother pulled her into her arms, gave her a quick hug, then set her apart, her hands curled around Blythe's puny biceps. "I watched the three of you last night from the kitchen window, playing with the dog. It's been a long time since I heard either Wes or Jack laugh like that. So thank you for that, too."

Blythe blushed. "I hardly had anything to do with——"

"Maybe a lot more than you might think. Or want to believe?"

Then, with another squeeze, Candace bustled off, leaving Blythe to gawk after her. On the one hand, she supposed the woman's assumption—that what she'd witnessed was somehow Blythe's doing—was flattering, in a way, considering her obvious affection for her dead daughter-in-law. On the other, however...

With a sharp shake of her head, Blythe returned to the task at hand, which was to finish up the last few details in the room. It'd been years since she'd been this hands-on with a project that wasn't in her own house, and she'd enjoyed it a lot more than she probably should have...despite the unexpected, and unwelcome, complication of all that electricity between her and Wes. Yes, even during the aforementioned conversation last night.

Okay, especially then.

And her thoughts would keep boomeranging back to that pesky business, wouldn't they?

Sigh.

Wes had probably thought she was angry when she'd stormed off last night like some nose-out-of-joint adolescent. Not that she hadn't been, but more at herself than him. Because her huffy exit had far less to do with his nailing her neurosis than it did with her breath-stealing, hoohah-quivering desire for him to nail her.

So sad.

And the sorriest thing in a giant tote bag of sorry was that, had this not been Wes—widowed, still grieving, Congressman Wes whose son happened to be her younger cousin's BFF—Blythe might've relaxed the sex ban. Or at least been mightily tempted. If his *gaze* was that penetrating, just imagine...

And oh, she could.

However.

She was not so blinded by what even she had to admit was raging lust that she couldn't see the *more* behind his heated gaze. That as much as she might want to fool herself that this was about neglected hormones—on both their parts—that wasn't all that was going on here. Also on both their parts. Human connections were weird. They either happened or they didn't, and logic rarely played much of a role. Emotional neediness, however—pushy, arrogant, willing to do whatever it took—was real good at taking center stage, even if it didn't have anywhere near the stamina required for an extended run.

Which was why she'd split last night. For both their sakes. And now that she'd sorted it all out in her head—and completed Jack's room—she was back in control and all was well—

Blythe felt the faint shift of air current as the front door opened, then heard the dog barking and Wes's laughter, feet stomping up stairs, and her heart boinged into her throat. She checked her watch, truly startled to see how late it was, and her fight-or-flight instinct kicked in hard enough to make her head hurt.

Sunburned and scowling, Jack burst into the room, followed closely by his dad, all solid and whatnot underneath his pale blue polo and khakis. Wes gave a long, appreciative whistle—at the room—followed by the Dimples. "This is amazing," he said, angling himself slightly to take it all in. "The room looks twice as big—how did you do that?"

A simple question, compounded exponentially by the look in Wes's eyes, a cross between appreciation and invitation. Deadly, that. Especially since all her life, she'd wanted someone to look at her like that. Like she mattered. Except now that someone was, she didn't dare believe it, let alone trust it. Or, God forbid, act on it—

"Raising the bed helped," she said, wrenching herself from that way-too-trenchant gaze to focus on Jack, silently traversing the room. Too silently. Not the reaction she'd hoped for. "And the dark walls seem to recede. Time-honored design trick." She plugged her hands into her capri pockets. "So what do you think, Jack?"

At the boy's continued silence, his father prodded, "Jack?"

A furtive glance, a quick shrug preceded, "Can I go get something to eat? I'm starved—"

"You ate an hour ago," Wes said. "I think you can hold off for a few more minutes. Don't you have something to say to Blythe?"

"Yeah." The boy's gaze swung to hers. "C'n we paint it lighter?"

Oh, dear. Blythe thought Wes's eyebrows were going to fly off his head. "For heaven's sake, Jack—*you* chose the paint color! Not to mention helped put it on the walls—"

"I didn't know it would look like this!" His sun-scorched cheeks went even redder. "It's, it's like a cave in here!"

"It's okay, Wes," Blythe said before the obviously mortified man blew a gasket, even as she reminded herself not to take it personally, that heaven knew she was no stranger to clients' changing their minds. Even those not old enough to drive. Still, she'd thought she'd scored big with this one. The disappointment that she hadn't was hitting her harder than she would've expected.

Except…as Wes had pointed out, the kid had seen the room when it was nearly finished and didn't seem to have a problem with the paint color then. So why now? Her antenna went up, that something was going on here that had nothing to do with the color of the walls. And in any case…

"If you want to change the paint color," she said, "that's up to you. And your dad. It's your room, after all, I want you to be happy with it. But I have work back in Washington the rest of the week, so I can't do it myself. I can recommend a painter in the area, though, if you like—"

"Forget it," Wes said, his arms folded over his chest. "This was your pick, Jack. And Blythe spent a lot of time designing the rest of the room around it. So I'm afraid you're going to have to live with it. For a while, anyway."

"That sucks!"

"Jack! Apologize. Right now."

"Sorry," the kid muttered, then ran from the room, the dog on his heels, leaving a thick, airless silence in his wake.

Wes pushed out a weighty sigh. "I'm sorry, he's been like this since last night. In fact, we came home early before he said or did something that might cost me the next election."

The way his mouth ticked up at the one corner told Blythe he was only kidding about that last part. But the droop to his shoulders when he palmed the ladder leading to the raised bed told another story entirely. And her heart twisted, at how hard it must be when you wanted to do the right thing but had no earthly idea what that was.

"It's okay—"

"It's *not* okay, dammit!" Wes slammed his hand against the ladder rung. "This blowing hot and cold thing, it's making me nuts. Especially since I have no idea what to do about it."

She wasn't sure which touched her more, that he'd confirmed her suspicions, or his trusting her enough to admit it. "There's nothing you *can* do, Wes. Between his rising hormones and the grief—"

"It's been nearly two y-years, for godssake."

She gave him a moment to look away, compose himself. To keep *her*self from wrapping her arms around him and drawing his head to her paltry little bosom. "And it feels like yesterday, doesn't it?"

His head whipped around, his eyes dark. Close enough to crack her heart a little more. Then he walked over to the photographs, black-and-white prints in white frames. At the one of the three of them—it had nearly killed Blythe to frame it, but she knew it only made things worse to pretend nothing had happened, to deprive it of air—Wes stopped, staring. "Sometimes," he said softly. "And I hate it."

Again, she ached to touch him. To comfort in that most basic of ways. "I can't imagine how hard this is for you and Jack." She forced herself to look at one of the photographs of the three of them, at the pretty brunette with the laughing eyes, her arms looping Jack's shoulders from behind. "Kym obviously loved you both very much."

"Yeah. She did." His gaze lingered on the photo for a moment before he turned again, the longing in his gaze spurring her to gather her things and start toward the door. Wes smiled, then sighed. "Even so," he said, following her onto the landing. "There was no cause for Jack to be rude."

She hesitated, making sure they were still alone before saying, "That was the fear talking. Not him." When Wes frowned, she added, "You do realize he sees me as a threat?"

They were standing close. Too close. Close enough to smell him, to see the brown flecks in the green eyes now grazing hers. "And you're sure he has nothing to worry about, right?" he said, his voice gravelly, and she thought, *Stop that, dammit!*

"Nothing at all," she pushed out, even as she heard *liarliarliar* pinging around in her brain.

"Just checking." Then, flashing those damn dimples, he gestured for her to start down the stairs. "And no matter what my kid says—or doesn't say—you did a terrific job. So thank you."

"You're welcome—"

"I don't suppose you'd like to stay for dinner?"

For the love of Mike…was the man deaf? Her hand on the banister, Blythe turned, refusing to buckle at the hope in his eyes. And the kindness. Oh, Lord, save her from the kindness. "Thanks. But I don't think that's a good idea."

"No," Wes said on a breath. "I suppose not."

And hand her a bleeping medal for sticking to her guns, for not caving to the many, many little voices whispering in her ear to give the man what he so obviously wanted. Except what he really wanted, she couldn't give him.

Which they both knew.

So they continued down the stairs, Wes scooting in front of her when they reached the bottom to open the front door. A rain-scented breeze swept in, stippling her cheeks with moisture. Heightening his scent. Man had the friskiest pheromones on the Eastern Seaboard. Damn him.

"Send me your bill?" he said.

"Of course." Even though she had no intention of doing

any such thing, since he'd paid for all the materials and, in this case, she considered her time a gift—

She nearly fell over backward when Wes cupped her shoulder, then leaned over to kiss her cheek. Although by the time it registered, it was over, and he was standing there smiling at her. *For* her, she realized, a smile unlike the ones he bestowed on his son, or his constituents, or his parents. Not that she could describe it, but she sure as shootin' could feel it. All the way to her toes and beyond.

"Have a good night," he said, and she nodded and mumbled something inane before scurrying down the brick path to the driveway and her car. Not until she was behind the wheel with her seat belt fastened did she dare to look back at the house, where, hands in pockets, Wes watched her from his doorway, gilded in the setting sun like some frickin' angel.

The car yanked into Reverse, Blythe backed out of the driveway more speedily than was prudent. But she had to get away, from those eyes, that smile…from temptation. Because this man…he was doing seriously bad things to her head.

Not to mention—*big* sigh here—her heart.

Wes stood in his doorway for several minutes after Blythe drove off, wishing he could take a firehose to his unruly thoughts, all screaming like a bunch of crazed Wall Street traders. Because wanting to make everybody happy was a bitch.

Although that was nothing compared with how badly he'd wanted to gather Blythe in his arms and simply…hold her. Let her know he cared. Give back even a little of what she so easily gave to others.

And in another life, another time, he might have done exactly that. Thrown caution—not to mention reason—to the four winds and pursued her, full-out. Unfortunately, this life, this time, was all he had to work with. And this life, this time, was already chock-full to overflowing with problems as it was.

His son's attitude currently snagging the top of that very long list.

Wes went back inside, shutting the door behind him and following the beeps and boops to the family room. Finding the kid wasn't difficult. Knowing what to say, however, he thought as he leaned against the doorjamb, watching him, was something else again. That had been Kym's purview, Wes more than content to be his wife's yes-man. Not that they didn't decide as a team how to handle whatever issues arose, but she had always been better at finding the words than Wes. Just as she was better at decorating—their talents had been complementary, not competing.

Funny how Blythe, too, seemed to share so many of Kym's attributes—her eye for what looked good, her intuitive understanding of how kids' minds worked. And yet could there be two more radically different women?

And could his thoughts be any further off track?

Casually, Wes pushed himself away from the door and into the room, taking a few deep breaths to center himself. Confronting his political opponents—no problem. Treading that fine line between valuing his kid's feelings and not taking any crap, however...

"Hey," Wes said, dropping onto the sofa next to him. But not too close.

Jack's eyes cut to his, then back to the screen as he jerked his head to get his hair out of his eyes. "Hey."

"You get your snack?"

"Yeah. Grandma made brownies. She and Grandpa went to the store, she said to tell you." Another glance, another head jerk. A haircut was definitely in order. "Did Blythe leave?"

"Mmm-hmm." His arms over his chest, Wes pretended to watch the game. "You should write her a thank-you note. For the room."

"Um…didn't you already tell her thanks?"

"Of course. But it's not my room." Wes shifted enough to see Jack's face. "It's called being courteous. And I know you're acquainted with the concept, since I also know your mother made you write thank-you notes. And while you're at it—" He faced the screen again. "You can apologize for your behavior."

At that, Jack's head swung around, his expression priceless. "I told her I was sorry!"

"Did you mean it?"

Blond brows crashed over his nose. "You told me to say it. So I did. But you can't control how I feel."

Testing, Wes thought this was called. Common side effect of the hormones, even without the leftover grief tainting his mood. Wes's mother made no bones about how much Wes drove her and his dad crazy during this period, even though she could laugh about it now. Then, however, he didn't remember a whole lot of laughter. In fact, as he recalled he was pretty much a huge pain in the butt.

Still, if Jack didn't learn how to rein in his feelings— and his mouth—now, heaven help them all later.

"You're right, I can't," Wes said mildly. His father had never been a yeller, which as a kid Wes had found weirdly unsettling. Hard to argue against reasonableness. An example he had no qualms whatsoever about using to his advantage with his own son. "And if something's bugging you, you come and talk about it with me, and we'll figure it out together. But no matter what else is going on, or has happened—" still holding on to his calm, he turned to Jack

"—I won't tolerate your being disrespectful. To anyone. For any reason. And considering how Blythe bent over backward to make sure you had a say in everything she did—"

"It just didn't turn out the way I thought it would, okay?" Jack said, sagging into the corner of the couch, the cushions swallowing up the little boy who still peeked out from time to time from underneath the shaggy hair.

"That's not Blythe's fault," Wes said, which got a muttered reply he didn't quite get. "What did you say?"

"Nothing."

"Jack. Don't do this—"

"I *said*—" The kid jumped up, his eyes glistening as he slammed the controller against the cushion so hard it bounced. "It figures you'd take her side instead of mine!"

Then he rocketed from the room, stumbling over the poor dog, who scrambled to his feet with a "What just happened?" look on his face. Wes held out his hand and the dog plodded over to plop his head on Wes's leg, his tail slowly wagging.

"Not something you'll ever have to worry about, boy," Wes sighed out as he scratched behind the beast's ear. Then he sagged against the sofa back, his gaze landing on the family portrait mounted over the stone fireplace, from when Jack had been a chubby, grinning toddler, sitting on his proud mama's lap, and the future was bright and endless and full of promise.

And his throat tightened.

"So, two things," Quinn announced to the room at large as, in a bizarre combination of mismatched tops and leggings that only an eleven-year-old could pull off, she flounced into the inn's kitchen on that bright and sunny May morning. "One—" She swung open the gargantuan fridge door and pulled out a personal-sized bottle of grape juice, then heaved herself onto the stool next to Blythe and twisted off the cap. "Is it okay if I invite Jack as my 'date' to the wedding?"

Seated shoulder to shoulder beside April and poring over their cousin's vast collection of floral arrangement photos, Mel frowned at her daughter. "Excuse me? *Date?*"

"What*ever*. Can I?"

"Oh, I suppose. Especially since we already invited his dad and grandparents, anyway."

Blythe's stomach did a little jump. "You did?"

"Kids are already joined at the hip, so it seemed expedient," Mel said with a shrug. And a sly little grin that made Blythe want to smack something. Like, say, her cousins. Since April's grin matched Mel's.

"And two—" Totally unaware of the imminent smackdown, Quinn turned to Blythe, her hands clasped under her chin. "Could you please, please, *please* help chaperone our field trip to Washington two weeks from Wednesday?"

"Me? What about the person who gave birth to you? Or April?"

"I already asked them. Turns out the inn's booked solid that week. So you're my last shot. And anyway, *you're* actually cool."

Blythe frowned at Mel. "This doesn't offend you?"

"That my daughter would rather *see* me in the Smithsonian than be seen *with* me there? Nope. Besides which the idea of herding a bunch of teenyboppers around D.C. makes my eyes cross." She held up a picture. "And I still like daisies—"

"Forget it," Blythe and April said in unison before April peered around Mel to say to Quinn, "And I'm with Mel on that one. Not that I don't think the *world* of you and Jack, sugar, but I've seen your class. Half of those kids are taller'n I am. No, Blythe's definitely the right one for the job."

Blythe's mouth pulled in a tight grin. "Even if I was the third choice?"

"Please, Blythe?" Quinn said, curls bobbing as she bounced in place. "Otherwise Cheyenne Miller said she'd ask her mother, and let me tell you—*that* would be a fiasco."

"And why is that?" Blythe asked as April slid off the barstool to make tracks toward the small bathroom off the kitchen. For the third time that morning. Which, apparently, Mel had noticed as well, given her raised eyebrows at Blythe.

An oblivious Quinn huffed a sigh as Blythe found herself facing down something that looked an awful lot like the green-eyed monster. What the hell? *You, out,* she mentally commanded. *Now—*

"Okay," the kid said, "so Cheyenne's mom is divorced from her dad, right? And our civics teacher—Mr. Corey, he's the one taking us to D.C.—is single, too. And whenever there's like a parents' day at school or something—ohmigod, it's so gross, the way she's, like, all over him."

"I've seen the woman in action," Mel said, flipping a page. "It really is gross. Like a hawk swooping in on a dove. An aging, sad, pathetically desperate hawk." She chuckled. "On a very young, pathetically clueless dove."

"Seriously," Quinn said. "She even has these fake nails that look like talons." She shuddered. "Anyway, so Mr. Corey was saying we needed to rotate the parents, so the 'burden'—" she made air quotes "—wouldn't fall on one or two people. But it's like *so* obvious that what he was really doing was pleading for someone else to volunteer so he wouldn't have to watch his back the whole time." She curled her fingers, miming claws, then shook her head.

"Not to mention poor Cheyenne is mortified to pieces. Woman is brutal, I tell you. *Brutal*—"

"Okay, okay, I'll do it," Blythe said, laughing, even though she could still see the monster out of the corner of her eye, lurking. Biding its time. "Anything to save poor Mr. Corey from Cheyenne's mother."

On the island in front of them, Mel's phone rang. Quinn picked it up, glanced at the display and handed it to her mother. "It's Ryder. *Again*."

Grinning, Mel clamped the phone to her ear and disappeared through the swinging door leading to the dining room. The monster chuckled; Blythe ignored it. Sort of. She smiled for her younger cousin. "Tell you what—I'll even make a reservation at my favorite restaurant for you guys for lunch. Everybody likes Italian, right?"

"Well, yeah, I guess, but...*all* of us?"

"Yes, all of you—"

"Can we ask Jack's dad, too?"

Mouth agape, Blythe blinked stupidly. Good God—had the wedding crazies afflicted everybody in the family? Bad enough that her grown cousins had been dropping more than the occasional pointed comment about Wes and how there he was, all single and probably lonely and whatnot, over the past several weeks, but when an eleven-year-old joins the fray you know you're screwed.

Never mind that Blythe had taken great care not to even mention Wes since finishing Jack's room. Let alone seen, or heard from, the man. Not that she hadn't *thought* about him, but that little detail she'd kept to herself. And would continue to keep to herself, for obvious reasons. She'd been grateful for the break, frankly, hoping the time apart had given Wes a chance to come to his senses.

"We could invite him, sure," she said with a slight shrug, "but he'll probably be tied up—"

"Oh, no, it's okay," Quinn said, nodding so hard she blurred. "Jack already asked his dad, he said he'd love to meet up with us. He's cleared his schedule and everything. So lunch would be great!"

You little turkey, Blythe thought, then asked, "And when, exactly, did Jack ask his father about getting together with your class?"

And although Quinn's forehead scrunched, Blythe didn't miss the flush staining her younger cousin's cheeks. "Um, I don't know. Last week, I guess?"

"Long before you asked me to tag along, in other words." When Quinn lowered her eyes to the island, fingering one of the photographs, Blythe blew out a breath. "Even though you know Jack has issues with me."

The girl's gaze shot to Blythe's before she pushed a breath through her nose. "Right now Jack has issues with everything. And everybody. And frankly I think he needs to get over himself. You and his dad would be so perfect together—"

"Whoa, whoa, whoa…" Blythe caught Quinn's hand in hers. "And you, sweetie," she said gently, "need to back off and let people work out whatever they need to work out without your interference. Trust me, those things never end well—"

"Jack's dad likes you. I can tell. And you can't tell me you don't like him."

"We haven't even seen each other in weeks—"

"Yeah." Quinn's eyes turned steely. "I know."

Oh, dear. "You know, people can be friends without anything more happening than that."

"Because you don't want it to happen?"

"Or because it's not *meant* to happen."

"But how do you know that?"

"I just do," Blythe said. "Even apart from Jack's objections." At Quinn's glower, she chuckled. "Look, right now all of you have wedding fever. But strange as it might seem I actually *like* being single. Because," she said to the girl's frown, tugging her to her side, "for the first time in my life I'm finally giving myself permission to *be* myself. To be *by* myself. Find out who I really am. What I really want. I'm in a good place, really. A place without…complications. And I like it here."

Not a lie, for the most part. Hadn't been, anyway, before she'd met Wes and a loud chorus of what-ifs, like a bunch of noisy frogs, had taken up residence in her head. And, yes, between them and the monster it was getting quite crowded in there.

"So you're saying you're never getting married again? Or that you'd never even have another boyfriend?"

"Not necessarily. I'm not a fortune-teller. But I do think Jack's dad and I want different things. I may be way off base, but I'm guessing Wes wants, and needs, a wife as much as Jack *doesn't* want a new mother. And I can't be either of those things to either of them."

"Not now, you mean."

"No. Not now. And timing plays a huge part in whether or not a relationship works out." Not to mention, even if one were to set all the other objections aside, how the skeletons in one person's closet—say, hers—could, and in all likelihood would, wreak havoc with another person's—say, Wes's—goals. To your average Joe Schmoe, her youthful indiscretions might not make a lick of difference. To someone in the public eye, however… "And why are you so hot on this, anyway? It has nothing to do with you, really."

To Blythe's surprise, tears swam in the girl's baby blues. "Because it hurts me to see Jack so mad and unhappy all the time. I know what that feels like," Quinn said as she palmed her chest. Referring, Blythe assumed, to Quinn's own reaction to her discovery that Ryder's brother was her birth father, a secret her mother had been forced to keep from her. "And I can't help thinking that if you and his dad gave each other a chance…" She shrugged.

Her eyes burning in sympathy, Blythe nestled her cheek in her little cousin's hair. "You think that would fix things for Jack?" When Quinn nodded, Blythe gave her a squeeze. "Jack probably has no idea how lucky he is to have you as his friend," she said, then held Quinn apart to look in her eyes. "But it's not up to you to make it all better for him. Or me. And *as* his friend, you need to give him room to work this out with his father, and in his own time. You can't force things to go the way you want them to. No matter how well-meaning your intentions might be."

After a long moment, Quinn let out a shaky sigh. "I suppose you're right." Then her mouth pulled to one side. "But I still don't want Cheyenne Miller's mom to come with us."

Blythe smiled. "I'll still come with you on your field trip, if it means that much to you. But if Jack goes ballistic—"

"It's okay, I'll handle it." Then she threw her arms around Blythe's neck and whispered, "I love you."

"Love you, too, sweetie," Blythe whispered back as Mel and April both returned to the kitchen, giggling.

"Guess what, y'all?" April said, holding aloft a pregnancy test, the plus sign in the little box probably visible from space.

And the green-eyed monster started doing a brain-rattling jig.

Chapter Eight

Jack had been so mad when he found out Blythe was coming along on the field trip, he'd told Quinn he was too busy to hang out with her. Because it wasn't like she didn't know how he felt about Blythe. Of course, that wasn't the problem, the problem was how his dad felt about Blythe. Like the way he kept looking at her now, even though they were at opposite ends of the long table in the restaurant so they couldn't actually talk to each other—it made Jack's stomach hurt so much he didn't even want to eat.

Across from him, Quinn sipped her soda through a straw, her eyes all big and sorry. Too bad. The last thing he needed was some girl trying to run his life. Some pushy, smartypants girl who thought she knew everything about everything. Everything about him, anyway. About what he wanted.

Even though he didn't feel like it, Jack turned to talk to the kid next to him, some boy named Brandon who was kind of a pain in the butt, to be honest. But anything was better than having to look at that *traitor*—

"So," Brandon was saying, "I got this really cool game for my birthday. Teen-rated and everything. Wanna come over and play it sometime?"

"Maybe," Jack said, only half listening as he watched his teacher and Blythe talking a mile a minute to each other. Hey—maybe they'd hit it off and start going out, and his dad would forget about her. He glanced down the table to see if Dad was watching them, but Darnelle Freedman was too busy yakking his ear off for him to notice—

That funny feeling started up in his chest, the one that happened when he thought about Mom. All these people, laughing and talking, and he felt…empty. Alone. Like none of this had anything to do with him.

His eyes got all stingy, like he was going to cry; panicked, he shoved himself to his feet, the funny feeling getting worse. Tighter, like he couldn't breathe. He caught Quinn frowning at him, heard his teacher asking if he was okay.

He booked it out of the restaurant like a total dork, barely missing a waiter carrying a full tray.

Wes bolted from his chair, catching Blythe's concerned gaze, the connection—despite not having spoken to each other for a month—so intense it startled him.

Air whooshed from his lungs when he found Jack outside the restaurant, his face in his hands as he hunched over on the cast-iron bench in front of the window. Breathing out the adrenaline spike, Wes sat beside him, fighting the impulse to haul the raggedly breathing boy to his side. Kid was probably embarrassed enough. He settled instead for gently rubbing his back; Jack glanced up, then clamped the bench on either side of his thighs, gaze fixed in front of him. A woman pushing a jabbering baby in a stroller passed, then the mailman, who nodded in their direction before shoving a handful of envelopes through the mail slot in the door.

"You didn't have to leave," Jack murmured as the carrier continued down the street.

"You expected me to let you run off?"

"Sorry," Jack mumbled, then sighed. "But I wasn't going anywhere."

"Not a chance I was willing to take." Wes squeezed Jack's shoulder. "Want to talk about it?"

Not surprisingly, the boy shook his head, just as Blythe, trailed by an obviously upset Quinn, emerged from the restaurant. A breeze caught the hem of Blythe's ankle-length sundress, plastering it to her body, and enough longing winnowed through Wes's frustration to be worrisome.

"Everything okay?" she mouthed, sympathy flooding her eyes, and something even more insane surged inside him, an impulse to grab this woman by the shoulders and shake some sense into her, that she had every bit as much right to get good as to give it.

But now was not the time. So instead Wes nodded, then shrugged, as relief replaced the deflating panic that Jack hadn't taken off for parts unknown. He was right here where Wes could touch him, see that he was safe.

Blythe released her own breath, her hand closing around Quinn's when the girl reached for it, her mouth tucked down at the corners.

As well it should be, since Wes had gleaned from Jack's ramblings a few days before that Quinn had in large part brought about this little scenario. Her distraught expression now, however, mitigated Wes's annoyance. And under other circumstances he might have found her machinations amusing, in a 1960s Disney movie sort of way.

Then Quinn released her cousin's hand, creeping closer to squat in front of Jack, her distressed expression far too grown-up for her flouncy little sundress and sparkly flat shoes.

Jack jerked his head to the side. "Go away."

Wes cupped Jack's knee. "Easy, son—"

"It's okay, Mr. Phillips," Quinn said, giving him a tiny, contrite smile. "Because I know I messed up. I shouldn't've…" Wes saw her glance at Blythe, hanging back out of Jack's sight. Quinn faced Jack again, her mouth scrunched. "I didn't mean to make you so unhappy—"

"You really don't get it, do you?" He surged off the bench and past Quinn, stomping down the street. *"You can't fix this!"*

"Jack! For heaven's sake!" Wes caught up to the boy, grabbed his arm. "I know you're upset, but that's no reason to—"

"To *what?*" He spun around, his face reddening when he apparently noticed Blythe. "You don't know how I feel, nobody does! And *you're* not my mom, and…"

"Hey!" Quinn rushed him, staggering backward when Jack brushed off her touch. "It's not their fault, it's all mine! Be mad at me if you want, but—"

"Jack, honey," Blythe said, tugging Quinn to her side, "your dad and I haven't even seen each other since I finished your room—"

"I'm not stupid, for crying out loud! Like I can't see how he looks at you? Even if he hadn't already told me he likes you!" Wrecked eyes again found Wes's. "How *could* you, Dad?" he cried, his voice cracking. "How could you do that to Mom? To *me*—?"

The rest of his class began trickling out onto the sidewalk, chattering like a flock of starlings. Swiping at his eyes, Jack practically rammed his nose into a nearby boutique's window. Most of the kids barely spared him a glance as they moseyed down the street in the opposite direction, toward the lot where their van was parked. However, one gangly, grinning, obviously brave kid in glasses and a local band's T-shirt ambled over to Jack, asked if he was okay. Jack glared at him, causing the boy to back up, hands raised.

"Whoa, dude. Just asking," he said, then turned and loped away to join the others. Before Wes could take him to task, however, Quinn marched over and smacked Jack's arm.

"Ow!" Jack bellowed and spun around, clamping the spot where she'd slugged him. "What was that for?"

"For being an idiot!" Quinn said, her own arms folded over her chest. "I get that you miss your mom, okay? We *all* get it. And it's sad and awful, and I'm sorry you feel bad. But for one thing, if your dad likes Blythe, that's not a bad thing. Because you *know* you like her, too, and you can't tell me you don't. And for another, if you don't stop acting like the whole world is your enemy, that's how the whole world is going to treat you. Far as I can tell, I'm the only friend you have left, and I'm *this* close—" she pinched her thumb and forefinger together, an inch from his face "—to telling you where to get off. So you might want to think about that."

Holy hell, Wes thought as Quinn made tracks down the sidewalk. He looked at his glowering son, staring after Quinn.

"Jack—"

"Dad, don't."

"You going to be okay?"

The kid's gaze slammed into his. "Like I have any choice?" he said, then slogged off after his class.

"That one definitely takes after her mother," Blythe said

from a few feet away. "And thank goodness you were here, since I doubt Mr. Corey could have handled that."

"And I did?"

"At least Jack knows you care. In every way that counts." She hefted her large purse up onto her shoulder. "And I guess I'd better follow—"

"He's right, you know."

Questioning eyes met his. "About what?"

Wes waited until a hand-holding couple passed, then an old woman walking her poodle. "About how I look at you. What I said. Because I do like you, Blythe Broussard. I like you a lot. And all these weeks without seeing you hasn't changed that—"

"Ms. Broussard?" Mr. Corey called over.

"Coming!" Blythe called, then hustled to join the group, the hem of her sundress fluttering with some agitation as she walked.

Everybody but him, Jack immediately noticed when they got off the bus back in St. Mary's, had somebody to pick them up. And he'd told his grandfather like a hundred times he'd be back by six. He'd even texted him at lunch— before everything exploded in his face—to remind him.

He dug his phone out of his pocket, only to frown when he realized it had gone dead because he'd forgotten to charge it last night.

"Jack?" he heard Mr. Corey say behind him.

His heart banging against his ribs, he spun around to see him and Blythe by her open car door, both of them wearing don't-freak-out smiles. Quinn was on the other side of the seat, kind of hunched over so she could see him. Jack's face heated when he thought about what she'd said to him. How mad she'd gotten. How she'd hung with Brandon, of all people, while they'd been at the museum, and then *sat with him* on the bus for the ride home. But it served him right, didn't it—?

"Need a ride?" Blythe asked.

Frankly, he'd rather walk. Even though it was like twenty miles or something between the school and his house. He supposed he could ask to borrow her phone, but he didn't even feel right about doing that.

"I'm sure my grandfather'll be here in a minute."

Except he didn't know that for sure. And the idea of being alone in the parking lot gave him the heebie-jeebies. Not that Mr. Corey would leave him there, of course, but that was even worse. The man tried way too hard to be cool—

"Did you call him?" Mr. Corey asked. "Checked to see if he was on his way?"

"Uh…my phone died."

"Here," his teacher said, coming closer and holding out his own phone. "Use mine." Reluctantly, Jack took it—a new smartphone, wow—but then he realized he didn't know either of his grandparents' cell numbers. He always went to his contacts list on his phone when he called them. So he tried calling the house phone.

No answer.

With that, the fear he'd tried to pretend wasn't there made him feel like he couldn't breathe. What if something had happened to his grandparents, like maybe they'd been in a wreck like his mom—?

"Nobody's answering," he said stupidly as he handed the phone back to his teacher.

"It's okay," Blythe said to Mr. Corey. "I'll take care of him." Then she smiled at Jack as his teacher walked to his car on the other side of the lot. "I'm sure everything's okay, but you may as well hang out with us until you can get hold of them. Right?"

Jack's eyes darted around the lot, as if he expected his grandfather to magically appear, before he looked back at Blythe. How could she be so nice to him when he'd been so sucky to her? And Quinn—she probably never wanted to talk to him again. But as he watched Mr. Corey drive off, giving Jack a little wave, Jack realized his options were severely limited. Go with Blythe and Quinn, or stay by himself.

He swallowed. "Could you…could you just take me home?"

"Tell you what—we'll swing by your house, see if your grandmother's there. If she is, fine. If not, you'll come with us."

Still feeling kinda shaky, Jack climbed into the car's backseat. But behind Quinn so she couldn't look at him. And he couldn't see her.

The weather was warm enough to drive with the windows down. Meaning the rushing air was too loud for anybody to talk, thank goodness. He thought about asking Blythe if he could use her phone, but couldn't get the words past his throat for some reason. And anyway, he'd be home in a few minutes.

But first they stopped to let Quinn out at her house. She gave her cousin a hug, but slammed the door when she got out, her hair bouncing against her back as she stomped to her door.

After Quinn was inside, Blythe twisted around to look at Jack between the bucket seats. "Why don't you come sit up here with me?"

He did, but mostly because he didn't feel like arguing.

"Want to turn on the radio? Or see if there's anything you want to listen to on my phone?" She flashed him a smile as they drove. "Although I somehow doubt it."

"That's okay," he muttered, then looked out his window.

So she'd get the message that he didn't want to talk. Not that he could have if he'd wanted to, what with feeling like he was going to throw up—

On the console between them, Blythe's cell rang. She glanced at it, then said, "Would you mind seeing who it is? I can't answer it while I'm driving."

Jack almost choked when he saw his father's number. And got mad all over again. "It's my dad."

"Oh?"

"Yeah. Why's he calling you?"

"I have no idea. I swear. Go ahead and answer, it's okay."

"Dad—?"

"Jack! Thank God. So you're with Blythe?"

"Yeah. She offered to take me home because Grandpa wasn't at school to pick me up."

"I know he wasn't, that's why I'm calling—"

"Did…did something happen?"

"Nothing horrible. More like inconvenient. But I'll let your grandmother explain when you see her, I'm already late for a meeting. I'm just glad you're okay. And tell Blythe thanks for coming to the rescue. I mean it, Jack—"

"Okay, okay, I will."

"And by the way—it doesn't do any good to give you a cell phone if you forget to charge it."

"I know," Jack said, smiling a little. "I'll do it as soon as I get home."

"Good." His dad lowered his voice. "Love you, buddy."

"Love you, too."

Blythe glanced over at Jack when he replaced the phone on the console. "Everything all right?"

"I guess." Although he did feel a lot better now. Especially after talking to Dad. "Dad already knew about Grandpa not picking me up."

"Did he say why?"

Jack shook his head. "He said Grandma'd tell me. But that it wasn't anything bad." He paused. "Thanks for taking me home."

"You're welcome, sweetie." Then she chuckled. "I guess you're a little old to be called sweetie, huh?"

Actually, he didn't mind, even if he'd eat dog food before he'd admit it. But Quinn was right—as much as everything inside him wanted to hate Blythe, he didn't. Couldn't. Something else that didn't make sense. Like how, in spite of how confused he felt, he also somehow knew he could trust her. That she wasn't a fake. So he just nodded, like he agreed with her, because that was easier than explaining.

They'd barely turned into the driveway when his grandmother practically flew out of the house, her hands bouncing up by her shoulders. Bear came lumbering down the steps right behind her, barking his head off. Before Jack could get out of the car, Grandma motioned for Blythe to lower her window .

"And if this hasn't been the craziest afternoon!" she said as she bent over. "You got a minute? I just took a pie out of the oven and made tea—no, no, please come in so I can thank you properly!"

In the meantime, Bear had raced around to Jack's side, barking even louder and spinning in circles, like he hadn't seen him in five years. Laughing in spite of everything, Jack practically fell out of the car to throw his arms around his dog's neck, not even trying to dodge Bear's slobbery kisses as he listened to his grandmother's going on about how his grandfather had gotten a flat but hadn't bothered to replace the spare after his *last* flat, that he'd tried to call Jack but he didn't answer. So then he'd called her but she was outside and didn't hear the phone at first.

By this point she'd latched on to Blythe's arm and was practically dragging her up the walk, making him almost feel sorry for her. Grandma was intense. But Blythe seemed to be handling it okay.

"And as usual, I didn't have my cell phone with me—nobody ever calls me on the thing, so I never think about it! Anyway, I finally saw his message a little bit ago and called him back, but he'd forgotten I'd let Amy Patterson borrow my car for the day, since hers was in the shop and she's got all those children, so of course I was stranded, too. We knew you were on the trip with the kids, but neither of us had your cell phone number, and when I tried to call the school everyone had already left for the day. So then it occurred to me that Wes would know it, so I called *him* and told him what was going on, so he could call *you*." She let out a loud laugh. "I mean, it all worked out in the end, but my goodness—could things have gotten any more complicated? I thought technology was supposed to make things *easier!*"

By this point Jack had caught up, although it wasn't easy trying to walk with Bear dancing in circles around them. Over Grandma's head, Blythe's gaze slid to Jack's, her mouth twitching as if she thought it was pretty darn funny, too. Even if it hadn't been funny at all then.

"Everybody go wash their hands!" Grandma commanded as she marched back toward the kitchen, her elbows stabbing the air.

Jack ducked into the downstairs bathroom, figuring maybe Grandma would tell Blythe to go use one of the bigger ones upstairs. Instead, a few seconds later he was standing at the big sink, squeezing soapsuds through his fingers like he used to when he was little, when he heard Blythe say, "Mind if I join you?"

He took a deep breath, but shook his head to indicate that she could, anyway. She came up beside him, squirting the liquid soap into her palm before saying over the rushing water, "By the way, what happened in D.C. stays in D.C."

Jack's eyes shot to hers in the mirror. "Seriously?"

"Promise." She rinsed off the soap, then shook the water into the sink before reaching for one of the guest towels hanging on the rack. "At least," she said, her eyes on his reflection as she wiped her hands, "your grandparents won't hear it from me."

Jack turned off the water, grabbed his own towel. "None of it?"

"Nope."

Frowning, Jack scrubbed the scratchy little towel over his fingers. "Are you covering my butt because you like my dad?"

"No, I'm covering your butt because I like *you*."

This was crazy. *Blythe* was crazy. And exactly like earlier, Jack wanted to run. Except he was finally beginning to figure out what he wanted to run away from—the anger, the sadness—that was inside him. That's what needed to go away—the thoughts. Not him.

Or—and here was the weirdest thing of all—Blythe.

No, the weirdest thing was that they were having this conversation in the bathroom. But whatever.

"I don't get it. Why you like me. Especially considering…"

"You've been a pain in the behind?"

Jack reddened. "Yeah."

Blythe refolded her towel and hung it back on the rack, smoothing it out for several seconds before saying, "I guess because compared with some of the stunts I pulled when I was a kid? Trust me, you're a rank amateur."

He frowned at her, curious in spite of himself. "You were a bad kid?"

Crossing her arms, she leaned against the sink. "I sure as heck wasn't a very good one."

"How come?"

"Remember what I told you about my dad?" Jack nodded. "Well, after he left, it was like my mom...I don't know. Gave up. Not that I'm comparing my situation with yours," she said quickly. "But I was unhappy. And really, really mad. And I guess I thought by acting up, I'd get her attention."

"Acting up?"

"Getting in trouble. On purpose."

"Like what?"

She turned to the mirror to fluff up her hair, then looked at him again. "Not going there, bud, sorry. Since your dad doesn't know we're having this conversation. And what happened in *my* past stays there, too. But suffice it to say he'd ground you for life if you if you went down that path."

Jack almost smiled. "How do I know you're telling me the truth? That you're not, like, making this all up?"

"And what would be the point of that?"

"I don't know. Maybe because you think I'd think it was cool?"

"That I nearly got tossed into juvie? Trust me, it's not cool. And you wouldn't think so, either, believe me."

At that point, something in her voice, her eyes, told Jack she wasn't lying. "So did it work? Trying to get your mom's attention, I mean."

She shook her head. "If anything, I got unhappier, because I was doing things I didn't really want to do. And didn't feel right about. But I was desperate, I guess."

"Yeah," Jack said on a sigh. "I know what you mean."

Blythe chuckled, pushed out a breath of her own. "Take this for what it's worth, since heaven knows I don't have all the answers. But eventually, I realized not only that I *de-*

served to be happy, but that I was responsible for my own happiness. That it doesn't come from outside—it comes from in here," she said, pointing to her heart. "Once I got that through my head, things started to turn around. Not all at once, but enough that I started to feel good about myself again. About my life, and what I could do with that life. That I had a choice, to either be a Grumpy Gus or to find things to be positive about."

"Like it's that easy," Jack mumbled.

"Never said it was. It takes practice. A *lot* of practice. A lot of falling down and picking yourself up and starting over again, even when all you really want to do is smack something. Or somebody."

When Jack laughed, she smiled. "I had a lot of questions, too, back then. A lot of *whys?* Until I realized some things, there are no answers for. That the only way to get over the hurt is to stop questioning it and kick it out on its butt." She briefly touched his hair. "I suppose no one can completely *understand* another person's pain," she said gently. "But that doesn't mean they can't still hurt for them. And we'd better get out of here before your grandmother wonders what happened to us."

As they started for the kitchen, however, Jack said, "I still don't like the way my dad looks at you."

Blythe stopped, then smiled down at him. "Maybe what he's looking at isn't so much me as it is…possibilities."

"Huh?"

"Your father's still a young man, honey," she said. "And he misses your mom terribly. Do you really want him to be lonely for the rest of his life?"

Her words went through him like an electric shock. Because he hadn't thought of it that way. Even so…

"He has me."

"Not the same thing," she said on a quiet laugh. "And

anyway, you're going to grow up and have your own girl-friends, and go off to college, and then probably get married yourself…" She touched his shoulder. "If you want him to let you live your life, maybe then you have to let him live his."

A little later, sitting at the table and poking his fork into the still warm pie, Jack kept hearing Blythe's words in his head. About how his dad probably was as lonely without Mom as Jack was—maybe even more, since he'd known her for so long. And it wasn't like he didn't want Dad to be happy. Also, what Blythe had said, about it being up to him, how he felt? It made a lot of sense, actually.

Like staying mad at Quinn. Who was one of the most upbeat people he'd ever met. Even though her life hadn't exactly been perfect, either, had it?

Maybe he could learn a thing or two from her, he thought as he stuffed another bite of pie in his mouth.

Chapter Nine

Wes's Skype session with Jack that evening, during which the kid told him all about that conversation with Blythe, finally eased the tension in his chest from the day's events… only to replace it with tension of another sort. Or rather, intensify that which had already been there.

An achy, but not entirely unpleasant sort of tension, the kind that results from a combination of good, old-fashioned sexual desire and—the real kicker—the realization that, if even half of what Jack had said was true, now Wes knew he wanted Blythe Broussard in his life. In both their lives. Never mind that she'd made it clear she wasn't on board with that idea. But hearing Jack almost sound like a normal kid again…wow. Even if he backslid, which he probably would, this was still a breakthrough.

One that none of the psychologists he'd taken Jack to had been able to accomplish.

And, yes, he knew timing was probably part of it. That

Blythe had come along at the right time, said the right things, when the kid was finally ready to hear them. Except it had been Blythe to say those things. To face his angry, grieving child with the kind of grace and courage—and love—that few human beings possessed.

He leaned back in his desk chair, the after-hours silence, usually a welcome relief after the day's frenetic schedule, threatening to suffocate him. He glanced at the clock on his desk: seven-thirty. Early, for once, since he often sat in meetings until eight or later. His stomach rumbled, but the thought of the leftover, undoubtedly soggy sub in his minifridge did not appeal.

No, what didn't appeal was the idea of eating alone. Rarely had his law practice caseload in little St. Mary's prevented him from having dinner with Kym and Jack. The campaign had changed all that, of course. And then, afterward...

The ache ratcheted up to actual pain, of missing his son. Of being alone. Of a bittersweet gratitude for a woman who cared enough to be there for his son when he couldn't be... when it sure sounded as though no one had been there for her at that age.

He pulled his phone out of his shirt pocket, staring at it for several seconds before clicking through to her number on his contacts list.

"Thank you," he said when she answered.

"For?"

Leaning his elbows on his desktop, Wes smiled. Yes, despite hearing the caution in her voice. Because he also heard the smile, too. He had to be careful, he knew that, not to mistake kindness for attraction. On her part, that is. Not to pressure her into anything she really didn't want. But when Jack had told him what she'd said, about realizing she deserved happiness, it was as if something inside him broke. Hopefully for both of them.

"For that little chat you had with Jack today."

"Ah. Told you about that, did he?"

"Word for word, I'm guessing. You done good." Sagging back in his chair to watch the twinkling city lights through his office window, he chuckled. "A damn sight better than I sure could have, that's for sure."

"Don't underestimate yourself," she said, her voice swaddling him like a soft flannel blanket. "You and Kym did all the hard work, made him who he is. But it came to me to...to be honest with him. To share. To a certain extent, anyway. I didn't go into details."

"Well, whatever it was, whatever you said, you got through."

She laughed. "I sincerely doubt it was some kind of miracle cure. That kind of pain...one conversation isn't going to heal it."

Tell me about it, Wes thought, then said, "Where are you?"

A couple of seconds passed before she said, "Here."

"Here? As in, close enough to take pity on a lonely congressman and have dinner with him?"

"That is the sorriest excuse for a pickup line I've ever heard. And I've heard a lot of sorry lines, believe me."

"So I'm a little rusty," he said, smiling. "Considering my last date was in..." He counted back, then groaned. "God, I'm old. But unless I'm more out of the loop than I thought, I don't think asking you to dinner is picking you up." He frowned. "Is it?"

"It is from most guys."

"One, that's beyond sad. And two, I'm not most guys."

Another pause. "No, you certainly aren't. And if it really is just dinner..."

"I'm not speaking in code, Blythe. Not that I'm aware of, anyway. But I am starving and all I have here is…" he poked at the sandwich, as though making sure it was dead "…something I don't think Bear would even eat. Besides, buying you dinner is the least I can do. Considering everything you did for Jack today." At her silence, he said, very softly, "You didn't have to tell me you were in town, you know. Or you could have said you were busy. Or to go to hell. That you didn't do any of those things…"

"I don't suppose I could tell you to go to hell now."

"You could. But I probably wouldn't take you seriously."

Another of those warm chuckles, then, "If you're up for trekking out to Alexandria, there's a Chinese joint on Henry Street, near Queen. The Golden something-or-other, I've been going there so long I don't remember the name anymore."

Wes plugged the info into his phone. "The Golden Wok?"

"That's it. You know it?"

"No, but my phone does."

She laughed. "Meet you there in, say, forty-five minutes?"

"Done," Wes said, on his feet before the word was out of his mouth.

And grinning like a damn fool.

Wes wasn't there yet when Blythe got to the no-frills restaurant, the comforting scent of a thousand stir-frys welcoming her even more than the diminutive hostess's bright smile.

"One?"

"Two. I'm waiting for someone."

"You sit over there? I tell…her? Him…?"

"Him."

"I direct him to table when he arrive, okay?"

Blythe slid into the tan vinyl booth, reluctant to relax into its embrace for fear she'd pass out. She'd told herself she'd only agreed to have dinner with Wes because (a) she wanted to make sure Jack had gotten his story straight, and (b) she was starving. She really needed to do a serious grocery run one of these days. But by the time she'd dragged her weary butt through the front door, she'd done well to spread peanut butter on crackers, peel the foil lid off a container of yogurt. Even the thought of picking up the phone and ordering in had made her head hurt.

In fact, she'd already been in her jammies when Wes had called, sprawled on her sofa and half watching yet another talent show while awaiting a visit from the sleep fairy. Wes should only know what it had taken for her to actually get dressed—although she used the term loosely, she mused as she glanced down at the first unwrinkled top she laid her hands on—and haul her tushie back out her door. She hadn't even reapplied her makeup.

Lest, you know, he think she'd made an effort or anything.

Then Wes appeared, and damn if her breath didn't jam up at the back of her throat at how gosh darn good-looking he was. And that was before he spotted her and flashed those gosh darn adorable dimples, and gosh darn if her entire system didn't jolt awake. Like she'd mainlined a six-pack of Red Bull.

He started toward her, all loose-boned amble in his dark gray suit and blue dress shirt, his loosened tie.

"Is the food as good as it smells?"

"Better," Blythe said, and his grin widened. Dropping into the opposite seat, he tugged off the tie, then folded it to slip into his jacket pocket. And in the unflattering overhead light Blythe noticed the lines webbing the corners of his eyes, the shadows underneath them. Didn't make him less handsome—alas—but it did make him look more... real. And—alas, again—stirred up a whole slew of let-Mama-make-it-better feelings inside her. Except the last thing she was feeling right now was *maternal*.

"Tired?" she said.

"Long day, yeah. Although on the taxi ride here——" he grinned again "——I must've gotten a second wind."

"Taxi?"

He shrugged. "Not sure what parking would be like, not in the mood to deal with the Metro."

The perky waitress came, took their soup orders. Hot and sour for both. "Was it really only hours ago that we had lunch together?" Blythe asked.

"We had lunch at the same time, in the same place. Together?" Wes shook his head before his mouth tilted. "This is much nicer."

And scarier.

Oh, *so* much scarier. Especially when Wes's eyes barely left hers while they ate their soup and she filled in the blanks Jack had left out from their earlier conversation. But, of course, he'd pay close attention, they were talking about his son, and Wes was nothing if not a devoted father.

Then he shared his "theory" about her having accomplished a breakthrough or something and a bit of hot red pepper exploded in the back of her throat.

"Me?" she said, grabbing for her ice water, sucking a piece of ice into her mouth and chomping down on it. "Don't be ridiculous."

"I'm serious," he said, locking her gaze with his. More explosions ensued. And not in her throat. "The kid had wrapped his grief around him like a blanket in the middle of summer. And *you*——" his spoon jabbed in her direction "——got him to take it off."

There wasn't enough ice in the world. Especially since Wes was focusing on her like a student in a particularly hard class determined to understand the material. A realization that discomfited her even as it made her feel, well, as if he gave a damn. About what she thought. What she felt.

"If I did, I'm glad," she said, thinking she should have gotten egg drop soup instead. "Because I remember what it's like, when your anger feels like a twenty-foot-long snake thrashing around inside you."

"And are we the metaphor champions of the world, or what?"

She smiled. "One of my instructors once said imagery is one way humans make sense of their feelings. That we unconsciously translate…how did she put that? The ephemeral into the concrete. Sorry," she said to his frown. "Didn't mean to go all Psych 101 on you—"

"No, it's not that." Wes finished off his soup, setting the bowl to one side before crossing his arms. "I was just thinking I'm sorry Quinn got sucked into all of this."

"Don't kid yourself—she didn't get sucked into anything. She put herself right in the middle of it. And stayed there, if you noticed. She'll be fine. Not only is she one tough cookie, but she's got a very strong support system."

"I'll bet she does." He paused. "I don't suppose you guys rent out?"

Blythe assumed he meant for his son. Then again, judging from the heat in his eyes, maybe not.

Maybe she should dump the ice water over her *head*.

"Jack said he called Quinn," Wes said as Blythe's gaze shifted to the plate of egg rolls between them. Nice, safe noncombustible egg rolls. She grabbed one, ripping off the end to pour soy sauce inside, as the waitress removed their soup bowls and laid out way more food than they could possibly eat in one sitting. "To make it up to her."

"I know. She called me, too, very relieved. Tough cookies get hurt, too," she said, blushing again when Wes stopped in the midst of spooning moo shu pork onto his plate to meet her gaze. "But I gather their 'date' for the wedding is back on."

"Date?" Wes's brow knotted. "I know they're only eleven, but—"

"Have you actually talked to Quinn? Kid was born old. So I wouldn't go off the deep end. Not yet, anyway."

"That's what worries me. The 'not yet' part. Especially if Quinn…" Color flooded his cheeks, which was so cute Blythe couldn't stand it.

"Especially if Quinn, what?"

"Takes, uh, after her mom." He gestured in the general area of his chest. "You know. Physically."

Blythe burst out laughing. "Our last summer together, when Mel was sixteen and we all put on our bathing suits for the first time that season…let's just say Mel had blossomed. Our grandmother was horrified. Especially when we'd go strut our stuff—even though Mel was the only one with stuff to strut—on the boardwalk and boys were tripping over themselves right and left. And that's when Mel *was* wearing a cover-up. Man, I had boob envy like you wouldn't believe." She chuckled. "Still do."

"And how old was Mel when she had Quinn?"

"Um…seventeen."

Wes jabbed his chopsticks at her. "Exactly."

Blythe jabbed hers right back. "First off, you're going to make yourself nuts speculating about things that won't even be an issue until years from now. If they even stay friends. And what happened to Mel…" She shoveled fried rice onto her plate. "That fall she was hurting and angry about a lot of things, including her father's death. And Ryder's breaking off their friendship. Which Ryder's punk younger brother—who had sleazeball tendencies even as a kid—took advantage of." Shaking her head, she dug into her beef and broccoli. "Two entirely different situations. And relationships. And Jack is nothing like Jeremy."

"Even though he hasn't exactly been a model kid these past months."

Wes's expression cracked her heart. "But that's not *him,* Wes, that's his pain. As opposed to Jeremy, who, unless he's had a come-to-Jesus moment I don't know about, simply isn't a very nice person. At heart Jack's a good kid. And Quinn's his best friend. If he's already apologized for today..." She shook her head. "I sincerely doubt he'd ever hurt her. Not deliberately. And knowing Quinn," she said with a smile, "I sincerely doubt she'd give him the chance."

Although one side of his mouth hiked up, he still sighed. "But hormones—"

"Are the devil's handiwork. Believe me, nobody knows that better than I do. I'm not saying turn a blind eye. But I do think it's a little early to get your boxers in a bunch. Mel's keeping an eagle eye out—trust me."

There went that crooked smile again. "In other words, one wrong move and Jack's—"

"Dead meat. You got it."

And he laughed, his eyes crinkling at the corners, the sound warming her in places that had been cold and lonely for far too long. And dammit, it felt good.

She was exhausted, she knew. Certainly way too tired to keep her battered guard propped up, to fight against the soporific effects of good food and, as dinner progressed, a conversation that effortlessly shifted to topics not at all related to their original reason for getting together that evening. Because she and Wes talked as she'd never talked with another man before, about family and life and things metaphysical and philosophical, topics not usually covered during a first date, let alone a nondate. Topics usually reserved for "later," after the realization that this was something worth getting serious about, and someone to get serious with.

Or maybe just someone to take the edge off that chronic emptiness Blythe wasn't nearly as good at ignoring as she wanted to believe, that no amount of busyness ever completely assuaged.

And that month apart? Might as well have never happened.

So, a good two hours later, after Wes paid the bill, then linked their fingers as they started down the nearly deserted side street back to her place, she didn't fight that, either. Although he did lift their hands as they walked, giving her a questioning look.

"You okay with this?"

"Holding hands? Sure."

Then he turned her around, gently clasping her shoulders. A warm breeze sifted through a lush-leafed maple overhead, dappling them in shuddering shadows. "How about this?" he said, before kissing her so sweetly tears pricked at her eyes.

She backed up. A little. "Aren't you afraid someone might recognize you?"

Wes laughed. "Save for the random, obsessed C-Span fan, that's highly unlikely. And I'm in a risk-taking kind of mood tonight."

Well, then. Figuring if it didn't worry him, it didn't worry her, either, Blythe kissed him back, her attempt not to act like a woman who hadn't locked lips with a man in nearly two years not altogether successful. Smiling against her mouth, Wes cupped her jaw and kissed her more deeply—oh, dear merciful heavens, could the man kiss!—and everything inside Blythe got all warm and gooey and achy-needy.

Especially when his hands slipped to her waist, his touch so careful, so gentle, when he tugged her closer to kiss her again, tongue to tongue, and it was crazy and hot and wonderful and silly, that they were doing this at all, let alone in public, even though there was virtually no one around because it was so late. Was it absurd, how happy this made her, that she felt like some idiot teenager making out with the hottest guy in class, right where God and everyone could see her?

But while her idiocy status might still be in question, she definitely wasn't a teenager anymore—

Her hands planted on Wes's chest, she pushed away. "What was that for?" she asked, noting that he seemed completely disinclined to let her go.

"Because I wanted to." His gaze caressed hers, amused and sweet in the amber haze of the streetlamp, and the absurdity returned, nearly overwhelming her with the desire, the need, to be foolish in a way she hadn't in years. To be free, of her fears, her doubts. Her clothes. "Have wanted to for some time."

To give herself credit, she did actually think about what she said next. Weighed the pros and cons, even if only for a moment. The pros were pretty obvious, with getting naked and cozy with the kindest, sexiest man she'd ever known easily topping the list. The cons, however—that she'd be breaking her own promise to herself, that Wes might take it the wrong way—were nothing to sneeze at.

Then again, neither was his erection, importunately pressed against her as it was. All righty, then.

"And I'm guessing kissing's not the only thing you've wanted to do for some time."

"I'd apologize, except…" He shrugged. "I'm not sorry. In fact…" He bracketed her jaw again, holding her gaze hostage as his thumbs tenderly stroked her temples. "To be perfectly honest, all I want to do right now is make love to you until neither of us can think anymore. To fill up that empty space inside you." He smiled. "Literally and metaphorically."

When she gawked at him, he chuckled. "It's no secret how I feel about you. Now let me show you."

"As in…you want to come back to my place?"

He laughed again, so close she could feel the vibration. "Can't see doing this in my office, somehow. And St. Mary's is two hours away."

"Hour and a half, this time of night," she said, then took a deep breath.

He bent slightly to peer into her eyes. "It's still entirely your call."

"But you said——"

"Oh, make no mistake, I want this like you wouldn't believe. But only if you do, too."

His honesty was sexy as all hell. Unnerving, but sexy. But old habits die hard. Meaning, as much as she believed he truly cared, that his attraction was based on more than sex, she still didn't quite trust it. Trust him.

And yet…she wanted to. Wanted to believe, despite the thousand and one layers of cynicism shrouding her heart, that this man really, truly saw her. Not someone he found intriguing simply because she was so different from his wife, not someone whose own childhood enabled her to relate to his son, and certainly as something more than a distraction from his still-palpable grief.

But most of all, right now? She wanted *him*. Even if their immediate goals were mutually exclusive.

"And will you leave if I say this is only about tonight?"

A long moment passed before, slowly, he shook his head.

"Why?" she said, not sure if she was more irritated with him or herself. "Why, when I can't give you any promises—?"

"Because if I did," Wes said, grazing his knuckle down her cheek, "that would make me like all the rest, wouldn't it?"

Oh, dear God. Oh, *crap.* All she'd expected, when he'd called, was dinner and conversation. Not a freaking challenge. Then again, she could say no, too. Could laugh and thank him for dinner, then turn him around, pointing him toward the intersection, where he'd find a taxi. Except, if she did that, what would that make her?

She took his hand. "I haven't been home much, the place is a mess."

"Somehow," Wes said, lifting her hand to kiss it, "I doubt I'll notice."

He knew it was wrong, thinking about the last time he'd barely closed a door before clothes flew all over the room, when hands and mouths and those clothes tangled in a haze of need. But, as Wes pushed Blythe against her living room wall, illuminated only by the glow of the streetlamp outside, the memory briefly sparked at how similar this was to his first time with Kym, when they'd both been eighteen.

At least, the flying clothes, hazed-need part. As had been the mad dash into the grocery store for condoms ten minutes before—and can we give a shout-out for self-checkouts? But all the rest...night and day.

He'd barely gotten on the condom when Blythe grabbed his shoulders to wrap her legs around his waist, crying out her welcome as he drove into her. Except before he could pull back for another thrust, she clamped her legs to hold him still, her lips glistening in the dim light as she smiled.

"Don't move," she whispered, eyes and bodies locked in an excruciatingly exquisite suspension of time and space, giving him time to absorb the moment, to absorb her, before, on a sharp nod, her eyes drifted closed and her orgasm kicked in, then took off, inviting him along for the ride...a wild, crazy amusement park ride that left him dizzy and breathless and laughing into her moist neck when it was over.

Wes carefully set her back on the floor, pressed into her warmth, her nipples still hard against his chest. Their heartbeats were off-sync, knocking against each other. A breeze shunted across their damp bodies through the open window somewhere, making them both shiver. And laugh.

"This wasn't exactly how I saw this playing out in my head," he murmured, and she laughed again, then skimmed her hands down his back, cupping his backside.

"Considering how long it's been for both of us, I'm surprised we made it upstairs."

Except he saw the shadow in her eyes. The it-was-what-it-was, don't-overthink-things warning.

So he didn't. Didn't play the let's-talk-this-out card, didn't give her a chance to explain the shadow. Just grabbed her hand and tugged her toward the bedroom, groping for the switch that illuminated the shaded sconces on either side of the whitewashed headboard.

"Again? You can't be serious," she said as he chuckled at the unmade bed, the explosion of color in the small room. Not to mention the explosion of everything else. She hadn't been kidding about it being messy.

"You have no idea how serious I am," he said as eased her onto the rumpled coral sheets that smelled of her perfume. "Sure, that was fun and all," he said, bracing himself on his arms before leaning down for a kiss. "But as I said. Not what I had in mind."

"Which would be…?"

"Something involving foreplay." He kissed her again. "A *lot* of foreplay, actually."

"But…the light?"

He sat back on his haunches. Let his gaze roam until she blushed. And shivered. Which made those cute little nipples perk right back up. "It's okay, I'm good."

She laughed, then hoisted herself onto her elbows to check him out, then frowned back up at him. "Um, can you…? I mean, so soon…?"

"First off, I'm in no hurry. Second, I imagine by the time I'm done looking and touching and tasting as much as I want to, we'll both be more than ready again."

"Oh, yeah?" Her smile teasing, she laid back down. "Sounds promising."

"And I do not break my promises," he said, proceeding to demonstrate forthwith.

Letting her eyes drift shut, Blythe let Wes have at it. Have at her.

Have her.

Brother, he hadn't been kidding about the tasting thing. Or the touching. And here she'd thought she'd had some fairly good sex before. But this was like…like…

Like what it was supposed to be like. With someone who cared, that is.

Man, his wife had been one lucky lady.

And so was she, Blythe thought with a start when Wes stroked her to climax again—a much rarer talent than one might believe, if her own experience was anything to go by—then stretched out beside her to pull her close and kiss her. Slowly. Thoroughly.

Because, you know, it hadn't been mind-blowing enough already.

That whole up-against-the-wall episode in her living room? There were no words.

The same as there were no words—a few moans, but no words—when he moved down to kiss her in places it had apparently never occurred to any other man to kiss her. Cripes, at this rate she was going to burst into flames. And then rise up out of the ashes like a phoenix, good to go all over again, she thought on a low chuckle—

"What's so funny?" he murmured into her neck.

"Nothing. Just thinking."

"Thinking? Now?"

The combination of amusement and incredulity in his voice made her smile. And realize she wasn't being a very good hostess, letting him do all the work.

So, not being exactly petite, she handily reversed their positions. Judging from his grin as he folded his arms behind his head, he didn't mind. Lot to be said for a confident man.

"Women always think," she said, looking down on him from her perch atop his thighs. "In this case, about whether you'd like this more…" She brushed her fingertips over his flat nipples, then lower. "Or this…" His abs jumped in response to her touch. "Or…this…"

And, yep, something else jumped. Bingo.

Wes peered down. "Well, would you look at that."

"Oh, I am. I didn't really get a good look before, but… very nice."

"So glad you approve," Wes said, reaching for another condom. "But it's a lot more than a pretty…face."

"Honestly, what is it with men? Uh-uh-uh…payback time," she said, snatching the condom out of his hand and doing the honors. Nice and slowly, which produced some gratifying teeth-gritting and one very agonized hiss.

She fitted herself over him and began to rock, then

paused to lower herself, kissing him, letting him kiss her breasts, tongue her nipple as she felt him swell inside her, and she caught her breath, let it out on a sigh.

And he somehow sat up, still inside her, so that she was cradled against him, in his lap—

"I'm can't...I'm going to..."

"It's okay, I've got you." He rearranged them, his arms so strong and steady around her, his voice tender as he whispered, "Don't worry, I won't let you go..."

They climaxed in tandem, their combined tremors shuddering through her like a warm, gentle current illuminating every cell in her body. When it was over, she collapsed in his arms, reveling in the closeness, his heartbeat speaking to hers, a deep peace the likes of which she couldn't remember ever feeling before.

Momentary though it was.

Because, the fantasy now indulged, reality crept back out of the shadows, sneering and snapping at her consciousness.

That even if she trusted Wes—which she did, with all her heart—this wasn't only about them.

Tears biting at her eyes, Blythe took Wes's face in hers to lightly kiss him, then climbed off his lap and out of the bed, thinking that, sometimes, being a grown-up sucked.

Confusion knocked Wes's postcoital mellow on its ass as he watched Blythe grab a lightweight robe from the pile of clothes on her chair, then pad across the carpet to smack down the light switch, plunging them into total darkness. A moment later the window blinds jerked open; bands of lamplight streaked across the patterned carpet, the bed, Blythe's frowning profile as she stared out the window, her arms clamped over her middle.

His own forehead pinched, Wes hauled himself up on one arm. "You want me to leave?"

She laughed, the sound hollow. "Unfortunately, no."

He levered himself off the bed and over to the window, wrapping his arms around her from behind. "We're on the same page, then. Because I'm not going anywhere."

"Ever?"

Laughing softly, he kissed her shoulder. "Metaphorically. For the time being, anyway."

Wes's skin prickled when Blythe's forearms covered his. "Which is why you're one of the good guys."

"And this is a problem, why?"

Another sad little laugh. Then, "Dammit, Wes—that was the sweetest, the most incredible sex I've ever had. And I'm not saying that because it's been two years since my last…encounter. You really are good."

He tightened his hold. "Only because I had a good partner. We work well together—"

"Wes. Don't. This can't…we can't…" Her ribs expanded, contracted on her sigh. "You have to put Jack first."

Startled, Wes tensed. "Do you really think I'd be here right now if I wasn't absolutely sure you'd be a perfect fit? For both of us?"

Blythe turned in his arms to lay her hands flat against his chest. "Except you know he already feels as if he has to fight for your attention. I don't mean that as a criticism, because what you're doing…it matters. Which one day he'll understand. But he's not there yet. And I suspect he won't be for some time."

Wes carefully braced her long, lovely neck to skim his thumbs across her jaw. "You don't think the two of you got over a major hurdle today?"

"That doesn't mean…" She sighed. "I won't put myself between you and your son, Wes. Which I more or less told him. Fine, so you caught me in a weak moment, when…" Her eyes sheened. "When I found myself thinking, wouldn't it be nice to do this with someone who cared? But this, tonight," she went on, shaking her head, "it was strictly between us. A onetime thing—"

"Says who?"

He watched her pulse tick at the base of her throat for several seconds before she said, "I can't do this, Wes. Bad enough that I feel like I'm betraying Jack. But you don't really know me—"

"I know enough. That you're patient and generous and funny as hell, that you're smart and talented. And good with kids. That you get kids. And don't give me that 'I've got baggage' line, because I already know that, remember—?"

"Not everything. Because I didn't tell you everything."

He stilled. "What do you mean?"

Her breath stirred her tangled bangs. "The fall after that last summer in St. Mary's with the girls, I got plastered and plowed my friend's father's brand-new SUV into a tree. On the other side of his neighbor's yard. No one was hurt, thank God, but I chewed up their landscaping pretty badly. Not to mention the car. The judge gave me six months of community service, two years' probation. Fair enough, considering what she could have handed down." One side of her mouth lifted in a humorless smile. "Especially if she'd known about my other indiscretions."

She spoke almost dispassionately, like a reporter relating the facts of an incident that had nothing to do with her. And yet it was the very lack of emotion in her voice that made Wes hold her more tightly, kissing her hair. "Where the hell was your mother during all this?"

"In her own little world," Blythe said, her breath warm on his shoulder. "One which she seemed mildly pissed that

I'd disturbed, but that was about it. In fact, as I recall she simply retreated even more into her work, as if to blot out that she had a daughter at all. Let alone one who smashed cars into trees."

"Even so…" He set her back slightly to look into her eyes again. "How many teenagers do stupid things, or have a DUI on their records—?"

"Except that's the very sort of detail that gets the blood-lust going, isn't it? Sends the snoopers poking around, asking questions that plenty of people in my hometown would, I'm sure, be only too happy to answer. After all, we're only talking ten, fifteen years ago."

She pulled away to prop one hip on the broad window-sill, hugging herself as she looked outside. "As opposed to your squeaky-clean background. Oh, yes, I've read up on you, about how as hard as your opponent tried, he couldn't dig up a speck of dirt about you. That you and Kym really were the ideal couple, that you truly had the perfect little family. That your integrity is *real.* Kym…she was wonderful, wasn't she?"

Wes's throat constricted. Not only at the mention of his wife, but at Blythe's obvious self-deprecation. "Yes, she was. But I'm not looking for her clone."

A shadow swallowed her face when she turned. "And I'm sure as hell not that. In fact after a lifetime of 'safe,' I think you're looking for something different. Some*one* different. Maybe with a little more edge? I intrigue you, don't I? Probably even more so now that I've bared all my dirty secrets. Not that I'm not grateful for your kindness, but—"

"*Kindness?* Is that what you think this is?" When she averted her gaze, Wes sighed. "Honey—that messed-up kid doesn't exist anymore. And you can give as much credit to teachers or counselors or shrinks as you want, but you were the one who turned your life around. Nobody else. I don't find it intriguing, I find it admirable."

"And that doesn't change the fact that this is all new and exciting and fresh for you—"

"Just because it's new doesn't mean it's not real," Wes said in a low voice, the only thing keeping the lid on his temper his realization that all her excuses, tossed between them like marbles to keep him off balance, were fueled by one thing: fear. And that broke his heart.

A breeze made him shiver; he grabbed a lightweight throw off the end of the bed, knotting it around his waist. "So I've only had one intimate relationship. And maybe it's been twenty years since I last tried to get a girl's attention. But I haven't lived in a vacuum since then, for God's sake. No, sweetheart," he said when she opened her mouth, "hear me out. If I'm any good at all at what I do—and I'd like to think I am—it's because I can tell within twenty seconds of talking to someone whether they're genuine or trying to sell me a load of bull. And while I have no choice but to deal with the bull-sellers, I sure as hell don't have to make them part of my life. I have no use for fantasy. Or flings. Let alone the time or energy to indulge, either."

He squatted in front of her, taking her hand. "Your confession doesn't change how I feel about you—"

She shoved off the sill, backing into the room with her hands held wide. "Maybe you don't care about my past, but that doesn't mean everyone else won't! And they will dig it up, you know they will…"

Shaking her head, Blythe spun around, her arms crossed tightly over her stomach as Wes got to his feet. "I get that you want to find someone to fill the hole in your and Jack's life," she said, her voice more steady. "Which you both deserve." She faced him again, remorse littering her eyes in the low light. "But I can't be that person. And if you thought about it for two minutes, you'd know I was right. Because they'd drag out my past. Trolling for dirt is our national pastime. And what would that do to you? To your future—?"

"And aren't you the little optimist?"

"And, more importantly, what would that do to Jack?"

Wes stumbled over that one, but only for a moment. "What does your background have to do with Jack?"

Her laugh was dry. "Nothing. Now. But if we were to…" She stabbed her hand through her hair, then released a sigh. "I've seen the toll these sorts of revelations take on ordinary families, let alone ones in the political spotlight. Heaven knows I've tried to move on. Except not everyone believes that's possible. I'd also like to think Jack's finally to the place where he can get back on an even keel with his schoolmates. Start to, anyway. But if…if you and I *were* to get together, how long would it be before the other parents got wind of my background? And used that as an excuse to wipe out whatever damage control he's been able to do?"

"You're still getting ahead of yourself," Wes said, not wanting to admit how much truth there was to what she was saying. "*I* don't even know what my ambitions are past the next election."

"Of course you do," she said with a gentle smile. "It's your destiny. And you know it."

"Even if that's true," Wes said, his heart hammering, "you're still projecting. There's nothing saying that would happen—"

"And is that a risk you're really willing to take? For all those people who are counting on you? For your son?" She shook her head. "I spent way too many years living in the moment, convinced that there were only consequences if I believed there were. Well, guess what? Consequences happen, whether you believe in them or not. Like, for instance…" He saw her swallow. "What could happen to people I've grown to care a great deal about if I listen to my heart instead of my head."

His heart slamming against his sternum, Wes searched her eyes. "Are you saying what I think you're saying?"

Another one of those sad smiles cut him to the quick. "Told you I've learned to be honest with myself. And with everyone else, for that matter."

Wes briefly considered using the ammunition she'd just handed him to blast her objections out of the water. Except…he couldn't. Because no matter what Wes wanted, what he might personally be willing to risk, he still had an eleven-year-old son who didn't need anything more to handle after the pain and upheaval he'd already been through. Not when, as Blythe herself said, they were beginning to see the tiniest glimmer of light at the end of that particular tunnel.

That the person responsible for that glimmer could also be the source of more pain…

A particularly choice cussword popped into his brain.

After a moment, Wes closed the space between them and gently kissed her forehead, then walked back to her living room, the euphoria of minutes before disintegrating with each piece of clothing he thrust his limbs into. He heard her come to the door, felt those sad blue eyes on his back as he dressed.

"I'm so sorry," she whispered.

Checking his pockets to be sure he had his wallet and keys and phone, he looked back at her, his chest constricting at her ravaged expression. Dammit, if anyone deserved to be happy, to be loved, it was Blythe. But as much as it killed him to admit it, she was right. No matter how they felt about each other, no matter how good they were together or how good she was with Jack—how good she was, period—he didn't know how to make the pieces fit.

"I know, honey," he said over the emotion jammed at the back of his throat. "Me, too."

He'd never had such trouble walking through a door in his life.

Chapter Ten

"Oh, my goodness!" Hands clasped to chest, Penny McPherson slowly pivoted in her newly completed great room overlooking the bay, the seventies vibe given over to a symphony of burnished leather and quirky antiques against soothing pale teal walls. "This is…incredible. That's the only word for it, Blythe. It finally feels like, well, *home*. It truly does."

And that's why I keep doing this, Blythe thought, bending to accept the middle-aged woman's fierce, teary hug. Not for her own ego—too much, anyway—but to see the joy on a client's face at the reveal. She was pretty damn good at this, if she did say so herself. And what she did was to dig around in her magic toolbox until she came up with exactly how home felt for each person she worked with. Which fed her soul in a way little else could, she suspected.

Like working with the kids on the website, where she could give to others what she never had herself.

Yeah, the self-pity fairy said in an overloud, nasal twang that sounded frighteningly like Rosanne Barr's. *I think that's called living vicariously.*

"I'm so glad you like it!" Blythe said brightly when the weepy woman finally let go. Unlike that fairy, which had planted her butt in a nice, comfy chair in Blythe's psyche, ordering in Chinese takeout like there was no tomorrow and clearly not going anywhere. "But let me show you some things you might have missed…."

No, let me show you something things you might have missed…

Except Blythe hadn't missed anything. Not the way her heart skipped a beat every time she'd see Wes's interaction with his son, not his tender, unselfish lovemaking—which she could still *feel* weeks after the fact—not her near-panicked reaction afterward when she realized, despite her determination to keep her emotions in check, she'd fallen in love with the man. And how the hell that had happened, she had no idea.

But it had. And now she was in you-know-what up to her eyebrows.

You got that right, honey.

Shut. Up, Blythe silently ordered as she pointed out various details to her bubbly client, focusing on her work, on what paid the bills and gave her a reason for living and had saved her hide after Giles left and she was alone. Again. That she paid those bills thanks to a design philosophy not as much about aesthetics as it was about an emotional connection to the space. Her clients' connections, that is. Not hers. Some wanted tranquillity, others to feel energized. Some sought to break out of a stylistic rut, others to unabashedly embrace the past through repurposing family heirlooms or using the colors they remembered from a favorite aunt's house. She never judged, or questioned, their visions. But she did facilitate them.

Which led to her thinking, after she left the beaming Mrs. McPherson and was on her way back to April's inn, about Wes's house. About his late wife's imprint on the space, how it glowed with safe choices and serenity and contentment. Of how Kym had celebrated her contentment by cocooning her husband and son in that manifestation of her love for them.

And that was great, really. It was a lovely home, one Blythe would have complimented the woman on if she'd known her. Would've probably liked her, too, in that way one can't help liking genuinely nice people. But then there was Blythe's place, that conglomeration of flea market finds and crazy color combinations that made sense only to her, of furnishings that shot right past eclectic to schizophrenic. How content she was there, in what to anyone else would scream chaos. Because to her, that was home.

Chaos? Really?

Yes, chaos. An apt word for her life, if ever there was one. Not to mention her personality. *Nice* was not a word Blythe would have used to describe herself, although she did try to be kind. And compassionate. But she was anything but safe. And, although she hadn't said it in so many words that, even if Wes wasn't looking for Kym's clone, that's what he needed, whether he understood that or not. Someone to once again bring order and stability into his and Jack's lives, who liked things all matchy-matchy and neat. Not a crazy lady with Rosanne Barr parked in her brain, leaving goopy take-out boxes all over the damn place.

Sighing, Blythe pulled into the inn's small parking lot, almost dreading—between both her cousins' wedding jitters and April's pregnancy jubilation—spending the night there. Peaceful, it wouldn't be. However, since she had another appointment early the next morning in a neighboring town, it was expedient. And these days she was all about expediency.

Once inside what was now the bright, airy lobby, Blythe did some reveling of her own at the transformation she'd wrought with what had been Hoarder Heaven. It had been truly mind-boggling, all the stuff their grandmother had kept. Except, weirdly, relationships, Blythe contemplated as she crossed the patterned rug toward the partially open door to April's quarters. From upstairs, she heard the muffled roar of the vacuum in preparation for the day's new arrivals, but otherwise the inn appeared to be deserted—not unusual at one in the afternoon.

"Knock, knock," she called, pushing the door open.

"Come on in, I'm in the bathroom!"

Blythe followed her cousin's voice to her bedroom, where she caught a double reflection in the dresser mirror of April standing at the bathroom sink staring at herself, holding her stretchy top in a wad underneath her boobs, her other palm pressed against her still-flat stomach. In spite of yet another spurt of envy, Blythe laughed as she walked to the bathroom doorway. "A little early for that, no?"

"I know, I know." Her skinny tortoiseshell headband no match for her humidity-frizzed hair, April grinned at Blythe in her reflection. "But I'm so excited!"

"You also have a very expensive wedding gown to fit into. So I suggest you tell Junior there to lay low until after the wedding."

"Good point," April sighed out, then tugged her top back down before pushing past Blythe into her bedroom, where she picked up a wedding invitation RSVP card off the small desk in one corner. "You might want to sit down for this."

Her forehead pinched, Blythe took the card from April, only to nearly choke on her own spit. "How did you—?"

"Not a whole lot of Lynette Broussards in Harpers Ferry. And I only sent the invitation as a courtesy. So at least your mother would know what was going on in the family, even if she didn't want to be involved."

"I can't believe..." Blythe looked at April. "She's *coming?*"

"I know, I nearly fell over." She cocked her head at Blythe. "You okay with that?"

"I...I don't know what I am. She didn't even come to *my* wedding."

"Oh, sugar..." April grabbed Blythe's hand to pull her down beside her on the matelassé-covered bed. "When's the last time you two talked?"

"As in, did more than ascertain we were both still alive?" Blythe pushed out a short, dry laugh. "Never? I mean, I feel duty-bound to check in every couple of weeks, but..." Her chest seized, like a charley horse to the heart. Momentarily agonizing, but it would ease. "Does she even know I'm the maid of honor?"

"Yep. Since I told her."

"And right now I don't know whether to hug you or smack the snot out of you," Blythe said, and April laughed, her hand going to her tummy. Blythe averted her gaze, leaning over to set the RSVP card on April's nightstand. "So how's Patrick doing? With the prospect of becoming a dad again?"

"Oh, Lord, you should have seen his reaction. First his eyes got all buggy—" she demonstrated "—then his mouth slid up into this real *I'm* so *the man* grin. It was priceless."

Blythe smiled. His first wife having left Patrick and their little girl after he returned from Iraq severely burned, the war vet had found a real blessing in the bighearted April. "You tell Lili yet?"

"No, we decided to wait until I'm further along. Eight months is a long time for a five-year-old to wait." She giggled. "For us, too." Then, eyes alight, April grabbed Blythe's hands. "You'll help me do the nursery, right?"

Their grandmother's house had been an oasis of constancy for April, whose parents changed addresses more than some people changed their linens. So now, after buying out Mel's and Blythe's shares of Amelia Rinehart's estate, she wasn't about to let it go for anything, not even the man she loved. The plan was to add a wing to the old place, expanding April's cozy digs into a spacious family apartment. A room for Lili had already been in the works; now there'd obviously be a baby's room, as well.

"Absolutely," Blythe said as the spurt eased into a slow, steady drip. Even though she'd told herself a hundred times since her and Wes's après-dinner shenanigans that the constant, niggling pain was nothing compared with the inevitable heartache down the road had she not nipped things in the bud.

"Oh, honey…" April pressed her hands to her cheeks, tears glistening as usual in her eyes. Honestly, the woman cried more than three other women put together. Certainly more than Blythe had since the day she realized tears weren't going to accomplish squat. Not bring her father back, not make her mother *not* regret having her, not convince anybody to love her. "I didn't think it was possible to be this happy! I really didn't!"

Even so, Blythe had to blink hard as she yanked April into a hug. "And nobody deserves it more than you, cupcake."

Snorting a laugh, April pulled away, wiping her eyes. "Everybody deserves happiness, Blythe. Even you."

Blythe started, only to then remember that neither April nor Blythe knew about her little dalliance with Wes. Because she wasn't a total fool. The dalliance itself notwithstanding. "What? I'm happy! What makes you think I'm not?"

April parked her cute little hands on her cute little hips. "Being reconciled to one's lot in life is not the same thing as being happy. No more than loving is the same as being loved. Which you also deserve."

And apparently the wedding crazies couldn't hold a candle to wacked hormones. "And I'm going to let that one slide because you're pregnant."

The blonde rolled her eyes. "The baby's not in my *brain*, for heaven's sake." A finger jabbed in Blythe's direction. "And deciding before you're even thirty that you're gonna stay single for the rest of your life is just plain dumb, if you ask me."

"Not that I did. Ask you." At April's snort, she added, "And anyway, plenty of people choose to remain single—"

"Which is perfectly okay if it's a real choice and not because they're scared of getting hurt again."

For the second time in less than five minutes, Blythe felt like she'd been clobbered. Maybe pregnancy hadn't affected her cousin's brain, but it sure as hell had affected her *mouth*.

"Where on earth is this coming from?"

"From you, where else?"

"But I never—"

"Came right out and said how much your husband's leaving wrecked you? You didn't have to. Oh, sure, you tried to act cool about it, like it was no big deal, but that doesn't mean Mel and I couldn't see through you. You spend ten summers with somebody, you get to know 'em pretty well, learn how they handle pain. I cry, Mel gets mad, but you…"

April pitched forward to clasp Blythe's hands. "You tuck it all inside you. Just like you did when we were kids. The quieter you got, the more we knew you were hurting. Like you thought if you didn't give voice to the pain, you could pretend it wasn't there."

"You and Mel—you talked about me?"

"Heck, yeah. Because we were worried about you." April paused, then said, "And we still do. Because we still are. Since it's pretty obvious you're puttin' up a front. That hasn't changed, either."

Dammit—the gentleness in her cousin's voice, exactly like Wes's…they were all going to be the death of her—

"…remember how I almost lost Patrick for that very reason."

Oops. Blythe scrambled to pick up the thread again. "For what reason?"

A huffed sigh prefaced April's tucking her legs up under her, the way she used to when Blythe would gather them together to regale them with her exploits. Except now it was April assuming the big-sister role Blythe had relished all those years ago, when she took such pleasure in lording it over her younger cousins. Of impressing them. Or at least scandalizing them. All of it an illusion, to be sure. But an empowering one.

"What's going on with you and Wes?"

Blythe nearly wet herself. "What? Nothing."

"That's not what Quinn said." Then April squinted at her, like she was trying to suck the truth from Blythe's brain. Yeah, she was going to be a great mother. If a scary one.

"Quinn's eleven," Blythe said. "She's puberty-addled.

Besides, I haven't even seen Wes since the day we all went on that field trip."

Technically, not a lie. Since he'd even left her house before midnight.

More squinting. For a moment, Blythe almost pitied that little bundle of rapidly dividing cells in April's belly. Then her cousin sighed.

"How come you used to be able to do that to Mel and me and we'd immediately spill our guts?"

"Maybe because you and Mel usually had something to spill your guts about. Well, Mel did. You, not so much. Me, not at all. Not this time, anyway."

"I know you're lying—I can feel it in my bones."

"And what is this? Payback for all those summers I bossed you and Mel around?"

"Hadn't thought about that, but sure." April crossed her arms. "You know, when I walked away from Patrick right before Christmas, I really thought I was doing the right thing. That I couldn't be who or what he needed. 'Cause I knew he had issues he needed to sort out with his little girl, and I believed I was only getting in the way of that. But the truth was, I was scared. Of watching whatever we had fall to pieces, of getting hurt. So I ended it first. And praise Jesus the man came to his senses the same time I did." She smiled. "Because otherwise I honestly don't know if I would've had the gumption to try getting back with him."

"And I'm thrilled for you. All of you. I really am. But my situation isn't yours. Wes and I—"

Heat seared Blythe's cheeks. *Dammit.* And the thing was, she could have still made the save, finished the sentence in a nonincriminating way. But no, she had to trip over that *Wes and I* and do a face-plant right smack into that deep do-do she'd been so determined to pretend wasn't there.

And of course April was grinning to beat the band. "So there *is* a Wes and you?"

"No, April," Blythe said on a sigh. "There isn't."

"But...there was? Or could be? Or what? Come on, help a girl out...and where are you going, missy?" she called after her when Blythe hauled herself off the bed and through April's sitting room, past the furniture and artwork she'd chosen and out the door she'd had redone.

She fled through a side entrance out to her car, parked in the smaller, private lot in plain view of the bricked patio adjacent to April's quarters. On which her cousin now stood, hands parked on hips.

"You even know where you're going?"

No, actually. Which could prove problematic. But hell would freeze over before she'd give April the satisfaction of knowing she'd rattled her that badly.

Although, considering the way Blythe had stormed out of the house, Ms. Preggo had probably already figured that part out.

So, in a moment of *real* maturity, she yelled back, "None of your business," before throwing herself behind the wheel, barely hearing April's shouted, "Nobody ever solved a problem by running away from it!" as Blythe burned rubber backing out of the space, jerking the wheel hard to pull out onto the road.

Even though she knew that no matter where she went or how long she drove, the truth was right there with her, like the little plastic Jesus that always hung off their grandmother's rearview mirror.

You got that right, honey, Roseanne said.

Bitch.

Jack lowered his car window, letting in the tangy bay breeze as Dad drove him home the last day of school.

And thinking. Listening to his thoughts instead of running from them, like that one counselor he went to after Mom died would tell him. Except back then, listening to his thoughts made him feel like crap, so he avoided them as much as possible. Now that he was older, though, he'd finally begun to realize that ignoring a problem only made him feel more confused, not less.

Used to be, he loved the summer, when he and Mom would hang out at one of her friend's pools, or they'd go driving along the coast to poke around in the other little towns. Until the summer before Dad got elected and she was too busy working on his campaign to spend as much time with Jack. His eyes got all itchy, tempting him to think about something else. But he took a deep breath and let the memory play through, about the talk he and Mom had right before…right before the accident, when she'd said she felt bad about not being around as much, that she hoped Jack understood how important this was. That he'd see the "bigger picture."

Back then, he hadn't really understood what she meant. All he knew was, he didn't like how everything had changed, that even though she was still around she didn't have as much time for him. And Dad—he sneaked a look at the side of his father's face, wondering if he realized how much he frowned these days—had basically disappeared, too. Even before the election. Then Mom died and Dad went to Washington and his grandparents moved in, and basically Jack felt like everything had gone to hell.

Quinn, though, had hammered into his brain that things changed, whether you liked it or not. Sometimes it was good and sometimes it sucked, but if you didn't figure out how to deal with it you were going to be miserable the rest of your life. Quinn might be younger than him, but in some ways she was a lot smarter—

"Bear!" Jack laughed when the dog wriggled his big old head between the headrest and the door to stick his face out the window, propping one paw on Jack's shoulder. "What are you doing?"

From behind the wheel, Dad glanced over and smiled. But it was that sort-of smile he wore when he wasn't really there. It wasn't only that he looked tired. Because before, even when Dad was exhausted, there was always this bright light in his eyes. Like in his head it was always Christmas or something. Jack hadn't seen that light in a while, which made him feel bad. Because he had the feeling it was his fault.

"So where am I taking you again?" Dad asked.

"Eddie Sloane's house. He's a kid in my class."

"Where's he live?"

Jack told him the address, a place in town not far from Quinn's new house. Dad was quiet for a couple seconds, then said, "You still taking Quinn to the wedding?"

"It's more like she's taking me, I guess, but sure." He hesitated, then said, "By the way, we decided we should start hanging out with other kids, too. Before people started to make a big deal out of it. You know, because she's a girl and I'm a guy. Besides which, *all* she talks about these days is this wedding. What she's going to wear, who all's going to be there…" Jack shook his head. "It's driving me nuts."

Dad made a funny noise in his throat. "I can imagine."

The dog's hot panting in Jack's ear was also driving him nuts. He pushed Bear's head off his shoulder, as he pushed the next words out of his mouth. "Blythe'll be at the wedding, right?"

Dad turned onto the street leading to Eddie's house, looking like he was concentrating real hard on finding it. "Since she's running the wedding, *and* she's the maid of honor, I don't think she has much choice."

"Good. She's cool."

That got a funny look. "Really?"

"Yeah." Jack tugged at his shoulder belt, let it snap back into place. He hadn't even talked about this with Quinn. "I'm sorry if I messed things up for you guys."

They pulled into Eddie's driveway. Dad cut the engine, then twisted around to give Jack the weirdest look. Like he was trying real hard not to show what he was thinking. "What are you talking about?"

Jack rubbed the back of his head. This was harder than he thought it would be. Admitting he was wrong, that he'd been only thinking about himself. But he'd seen his dad and Blythe together enough to figure out that Dad really did like having her around. Like that night when they'd had the cookout, and then chased Bear around in the backyard, everybody laughing and acting all goofy and stuff? Even though it got strange later, for a while things had almost felt like they used to, when it was Mom and Dad and him. Like…like he was whole again.

What's more, Jack also knew Blythe liked *him*. Enough to put up with his craziness. Even enough to lie about how she felt about his dad, so she wouldn't make Jack unhappy. Took him a while to figure that out.

"You still like her?" he asked his dad.

"Yes," his father said after a moment. "But—"

"Then…it's okay." Jack sucked in a huge breath, feeling a million times better when he let it out. And a million times better than that when he said, "If you want to go out with her and stuff, I'm cool with it."

Talk about the last thing Wes expected to hear out of his son's mouth. And knowing what it had cost him to say that…

He grabbed the back of Jack's neck, tugging him forward to kiss the top of his head, then sat straight again. "And do I have the best kid in the world or what? I know that's huge for you, and it means a great deal to me. However…it's not meant to be, buddy."

"How come?"

He was hardly going to go into the conversation from that night, even though the damn thing had replayed in his head a hundred times since then. As had the incessant, futile musing about how—especially given Blythe's not-so-veiled admission that she was falling for him, too—they might still make it work. Only he was still drawing as much of a blank about how to do that as he had then. Too much potential for heartbreak. For everyone. So moving forward, as much as that hurt, seemed like his only option.

"Well, for a relationship to work, everybody has to be on the same page. At the same time. And we're not."

His son gave him one of those far-too-smart-for-his-own-good looks parents dread. "Is this about the trouble she got in when she was a kid? Because I already know about that—"

"Not as much as you think you do. And it's only partly about that." Releasing a breath, Wes looked out the windshield. If nothing else, he owed the kid the truth. Or at least as much as he could give him. "You know what Blythe told you about how her dad left?"

"Yeah?"

"I think that broke her, in a way." He faced Jack again. "It made her afraid to trust that people won't leave her."

"That's nuts."

"Not when you've been hurt as much as Blythe has."

Jack angled away, clearly trying to sort this all out. Then, slowly, he nodded. "She needs us, Dad. All of us." He looked at Wes, his expression so serious Wes had to hold back a smile. "You and me and Grandma and Grandpa.

Even Bear," he said, some of the seriousness dissipating when the dog gave him a stealth lick. "And I think—no, I know—we need her."

Wes could hardly breathe. Although he finally got out, "I agree with you. But it's not that easy. For one thing, as I said, Blythe's—"

"Scared. Got it."

"Not only for herself. For you."

Jack frowned. "Me?"

"She pointed out—rightly, I'm afraid—the likelihood of her background being made public. If we were to get together. And how hard that could be on you. Not because it would necessarily bother you, but it could some of your friends. Or their parents."

Pale eyebrows vanished underneath the shaggy bangs. "Like I'd care what they'd think."

"You might if you suddenly find yourself sitting by yourself in the cafeteria."

"You mean, like I already have been?" the kid said with a snort, then smiled. "Except for Quinn." Then he sighed. "So what are you saying? We should give up on Blythe because of what *might* happen?"

A thought that, especially when thrown in Wes's face that way, made his stomach heave. "I don't—*we* don't—want you to get hurt. Not when you've already been through so much."

"And guess what? I lived."

"Yes, you did," Wes said over a surge of pride, of love, for his child. "And I'll say it again—you are one incredible kid—"

"Just get her back, okay?" Jack said, then fled the car, the abandoned dog barking after him.

His head swimming, Wes started driving, eventually finding himself at the same marshy beach where he'd taken

Kym the night he'd proposed. The one they'd kept returning to after Jack was born, a relatively secluded strip of
land still within sight of the Bay Bridge, now softly glittering in the hazy distance. He let the dog off the leash,
feeling his spirits lift at the sight of the Lab streaking to
the edge of the water, barking at whatever shorebirds had
the misfortune to be in his line of sight.

Here and there reed-choked, sandy berms gave texture
to the otherwise flat landscape, blocking the view beyond.
As well as the dog, when he bounded past the nearest one,
barking at whatever, or whoever, was on the other side.

"Bear! Come!" Wes shouted, his loafers gouging the
sand as he picked up his pace to come to the rescue of the
hapless object of the dog's attention…

Only to come to a startled halt when he rounded the
little hill to see Blythe sitting in the sand, a fast food bag
at her side and her arms practically strangling Bear's neck
as she buried her face in his ruff.

"How on earth did you find me?" Blythe said, not bothering to look up when she heard Wes's muffled shoosh-
ing in the sand.

"I didn't. Bear did."

Wes apparently took her soft laugh as an invitation to
plop down beside her. Even though, in khakis and loafers,
he wasn't exactly dressed for the beach. The warm breeze
snatched at his scent, kindling memories. Regrets. Not for
what had been, but for what couldn't be. And yet, coupled
with the regrets was the most bizarre sense of…normalcy,
she supposed it was. Considering how they'd ended things,
this should be the Awkward Moment from Hell. That it
wasn't was confusing the life out of her.

Bear nosed the food bag, then gave Blythe a hopeful
look. She grabbed it before the dog did, held it out to Wes.

"Hungry?"

"Um…" He eyed the bag with pretty much the same expression as his dog, then grinned. "Actually, yeah."

Blythe chuckled. "I somehow ordered a burger the size of Jupiter. And fries to go with. Help yourself."

"Does this mean we're still friends?"

"I'm not sure what this means. Other than I bought too much food and you're here to eat it."

Wes hesitated for a moment, then took the bag, peering inside. "Wow. You weren't kidding. You sure—?"

"Take the damn food, Wes."

With the half-eaten burger freed from its foam prison, he dug in, groaning with what Blythe assumed was bliss. Bear's amber eyes fixed on the food, he planted his butt in front of his master. Still hopeful. And, now, drooling.

"This is great," Wes said, chewing. "Thanks."

"You're welcome." Taking pity on the dog, Blythe pulled a French fry from the bag, tossed it to him. "And that's Dr. Pepper in the cup. If you don't mind my spit on the straw." When Wes canted an amused glance in her direction, she blushed. "Although I guess that's moot."

"Pretty much, yeah. This is fate, you know." When she frowned, he smiled, looking so damn relaxed and so damn handsome and so damn unflappable she wanted to clobber him. Or kiss him. Okay, both. "Out of all the beaches on the Eastern Shore," he said, "what're the odds of us both landing on the same one at the same time?"

"So you think this is part of some grand plan?"

A fry disappeared into his mouth. "Definitely worth considering."

"Or you could chalk it up to coincidence. As most of the world would."

"I suppose." Clearly refusing to take the bait, Wes pinched off a piece of the burger for the dog, then dispatched the rest in three or four bites before picking up the drink. He took a long pull on the straw as he faced the sparkling, slate-blue water, the sky stippled with clouds and bobbing, shrieking gulls. Down by the shoreline, a teetering little sandpiper preened itself, oblivious to his spectators. Until Bear galumphed off to disturb the poor thing's toilette.

Wes twisted the cup back into the soft sand, then pulled up one knee to prop his wrist on it. "I didn't think anyone else knew about this spot. Kym and I always thought of it as our little secret."

"Along with probably hundreds of other people," Blythe said.

"True. But we never saw them, which was all that counted."

She nodded, then laughed again when Bear started rushing and nipping at the water rippling along the beach's edge. "The last summer the girls and I were all in St. Mary's, I'd just gotten my license. Nana let me take her old Buick for a drive and this is where we ended up. I thought I'd found heaven."

"That why you're here now?"

"Maybe. Hadn't thought about it." She forked her fingers through her hair. "I was at April's. My mother's apparently coming to the wedding."

If the non sequitur threw Wes, he didn't let on. "An unexpected turn of events, I take it?"

"You might say. Although at least I have a week to prepare. As opposed to walking down the aisle and seeing her sitting there. That would not have been pretty. Aside from that, though, April got on my case about...some stuff. I wasn't in the mood."

"For?"

Blythe felt her mouth pull tight. "Dealing. Which is so

not me. Not these days, anyway." Her brow knotted, she looked at Wes. He'd reclined beside her, his head propped in his hand, watching her. "Running...I don't do that anymore." Still frowning, she faced the water and said softly, "Or thought I didn't, anyway."

"And what are you running from?" Wes asked.

"All that *happiness*," she said, surprised when her throat closed up.

His heart breaking for her, Wes reached for Blythe's hand, wishing he could somehow fix that part of her she obviously believed was deficient. Because Jack was right—she did need them. Almost as much as they needed her. "You don't think you're entitled to happiness, too?"

"I never said that," she said with a sharp shake of her head. "And the thing is, I'm not *un*happy. Most of the time, anyway. I love my work, and working with the kids online. And being around my cousins again after all this time has been great." She smiled. "Even when they drive me batty. But for the most part I make my own happiness. And I sure as hell don't look for it from outside sources."

"That doesn't mean you can't accept it when it lands in your lap. Say, when you're with your cousins. With Quinn."

Her features softened. "Okay, I'll cede that point. But I sure don't rely on anyone else for it. Because that way lies disappointment. And heartache. Learned that the hard way."

Before either of them knew it was coming, before anyone could come up with a dozen reasons why he shouldn't, Wes sat up to cradle the back of her head and kiss her, slow and sweet. "And, you know," he said quietly when he broke the kiss, touching his forehead to hers, "I could strangle whoever shattered your trust so badly."

"But on the bright side," she said, "it toughened me up."

You really believe that? he thought, but knew better than to voice that aloud. Because from where he stood, she was one of the most vulnerable people he'd ever met. Her giving heart aside. "Maybe so. But there are people you can count on. Like your cousins, I imagine." His thumb stroked her cheek. "Like me."

Blythe turned to tug her long skirt down over her calves, her gaze fixed on the water. "And we've already been through this," she said on a long sigh. "It's not going to work between us. It *can't* work. That's nobody's fault, it just is. I can't change my past, and you can't change who you are. Your..." she waved one hand "...mission. Then there's Jack—"

"Who, by the way, told me earlier today that—and I quote—that he was cool with us going out." He smiled. "And stuff."

A blush swept up her neck as her eyes cut to his. "And what does he mean by 'and stuff'?"

Wes chuckled. "Probably not what you're thinking. Not that he doesn't know about 'stuff,' but I don't think that's what he meant in this context. The point is, though, his initial objection to you doesn't seem to be an issue anymore—"

"Dammit, Wes! *Why?* After everything...everything you know about me, why are you still interested? Hell, why are you still even here when you know this is dead in the water?"

"Because instead of telling me to get lost when I showed up out of the blue, you gave me the rest of your lunch."

After a moment, she laughed. "Really? That's it?"

"Then how about because, despite all the crap you've been through, you're honest and loving and decent—"

"Decent? Seriously?"

"In all the ways that really count? Absolutely."

The breeze snatched at her skirt hem; she tugged it down again. "I'm also a fraud, acting like I've got my act totally together when inside…" She let out another, much more bitter, laugh. "Inside I'm a mess."

"Yeah. You said. So why do you think this makes you special?"

Her eyes shot to his. "What?"

"Honey, we're *all* messes inside. There's not a single human being on the planet who doesn't put up a front sometimes, so people don't make fun of us, or think badly of us, or quietly make arrangements to have us locked up. You want to talk feeling like a fraud, trying being in politics. No, I don't outright lie," he said to her lifted brows, "but you'd better believe there are times when I wonder who the hell I thought I was to think I could make a difference. When I'm flat-out petrified I'm going to look like a fool. But ultimately it's not about what we feel, it's about what we do. And you…"

Wes shifted to caress her jaw. "I don't know many people who would have put someone else's child ahead of her own needs, like you keep doing with Jack."

Fear flashed in her eyes. "I don't need—"

"Of course you do, honey. Just like everybody else—"

"No, I don't!" Blythe said, trying to stand, yanking her skirt out from beneath Wes's butt. "Because *needing* is what always, always gets me into trouble! And when I'm around you, when you touch me, or—" she scooped up her trash, the skirt clinging to her legs as she tried to back away "—or look at me like you're looking at me right now, I'm so tempted to forget exactly how badly needing—heck, even *wanting*—always works out for me."

On his feet by now, Wes jerked out his hands. "So that means it won't ever work out for you?"

"I don't know! But now's definitely not the time, and you're definitely n-not the guy!"

His hands dropped. "Really."

He could see her blush from here. "Okay, I can't be that girl. *Your* girl. And stop looking at me like that! So, please—go find someone who won't be an embarrassment to you and Jack, who you won't have to hold your breath about, waiting for someone to hurl the truth into your lives like a firebomb! Because I would never forgive myself if I caused either of you more pain."

Then she spun around, fighting to keep her balance as she tramped toward her car.

Frowning, Wes plowed his hands into his pants pockets and watched her go, hardly noticing when Bear trotted up to him, nudging a soggy stick at his hand. Only after he heard the growl of Blythe's car engine as she took off did he acknowledge the dog, hurling the chunk of wood out near the shoreline before starting back toward his own car. Four, five times they repeated the game, Bear easily keeping Wes in his sights as they progressed along the shore. The epitome of doggy bliss, he'd bound up and present his prize, bound off again after it was tossed, his joyful determination unflagging no matter how often Wes threw the stick.

Or how far. Or what obstacles lay in his path.

Because that prize, by gum, was worth any amount of effort to retrieve.

Not that Wes thought of Blythe as a stick, he thought on a dry laugh as he desanded both himself and the dog before getting into his car. But she was a prize, whether she understood that or not.

And somehow it was up to him to make sure she did.

Because this campaign wasn't over yet, boys and girls. Not by a long shot.

Chapter Eleven

Soon, it would all be over.

But not, Blythe thought, glimpsing Wes as she started down the short aisle toward the flower-smothered gazebo, nearly soon enough. They hadn't seen each other, or even spoken, since that last conversation on the beach. So, as far as she was concerned, they were done. And yet, the way he was looking at her, his gaze riveted to her like he wanted to crawl inside her head, maybe not as much as she thought. Hoped. Especially when his mouth tilted in that half smile that reminded her way too much of…things. Things indelibly branded in her memory, things she wanted to forget and knew she never would.

Moving on, she thought, fixing her own gaze straight ahead, to the pair of nervously grinning grooms waiting on either side of the jovial, slightly paunchy justice of the peace Blythe had scared up in Annapolis.

Quinn, as well as Patrick's daughter Lilianna, were already in the gazebo, adorable in their fancy outfits, both smiling so widely Blythe half expected to see the sun glint off their teeth, as it was off the breeze-rippled water in the estuary beyond. Yes, it was a picture-perfect day, sunny and not too warm, the bright-blue sky having shucked its customary bay haze. Yes, she thought as she took her position in the gazebo, turning to watch Mel and April start down the aisle, the brides both looked as beautiful as she ever remembered seeing them. April even had a little cleavage going on, thanks to the wee human growing apace in her tummy.

And, yes, her mother was indeed present, wearing something resembling a real dress, and real shoes, her silver hair almost as short as Blythe's, her smile when she caught Blythe's eyes almost as pained.

Her cousins reached the end of the aisle, took their soon-to-be-husbands' hands.

"Dearly beloved…"

Blythe couldn't decide if she was more angry with her mother for not telling *her* she was coming, or that she'd shown up for her cousins' wedding and not her own. Actually, what most annoyed her was that she was angry at all, that Lynette still had that much power over her. Or rather, that Blythe still ceded her that much power. She'd thought she'd let go of the pointless resentment years ago.

Apparently not.

"…to join these couples in matrimony…"

Weddings always made her weepy, anyway, she told herself as she blinked back tears, as the ceremony progressed through the vows to the exchange of rings. Happy tears, for her "sisters" and their terrific guys, for the happy grins on Quinn's and Lilianna's faces. For the heartfelt cheers from the audience as the couples kissed, signifying the beginning of their new lives together.

Then she noticed Wes again, his attention focused on her rather than the blissful newlyweds. And the tears welled anew, dammit, for what she wanted but wasn't hers to have.

And wallowing, especially today, was not only as pointless as the resentment, but downright selfish. After all, happiness was contagious, right? So bring it on.

Sooner rather than later would be good, she thought morosely as she and the girls followed the couples back up the aisle. A fake smile stretched her cheeks, making her feel like a creepy, chiffon-clad clown.

Todd and Michael, the fabulous couple April had hired to help her run the inn, had insisted on seeing to the reception, leaving Blythe free to mingle. They'd thought they were doing her a favor. In reality, not so much. Especially when she turned to see her mother, like a drag queen but without the fashion sense, striding toward her, reminding her eerily of her grandmother. Despite having married into St. Mary's upper echelon, Nana had never done dresses very well, either.

Not surprisingly, Lynette didn't reach for her. Instead she stopped far enough away to respect Blythe's "space," but still close enough that they could hear each other over the din of laughter and excited chatter.

Fidgeting with her clunky necklace, her mother gave Blythe a strained smile. "You look very nice."

"Thanks." The embodiment of an elegant, Ethiopian prince, Michael swooped past, bearing a tray of filled wineglasses. Blythe snatched one, took a long slug. On an empty stomach. "Why are you here, Lynette?"

Once upon a time she'd called her mother *Mommy.* Until she realized the word actually made her mother flinch.

Something Blythe couldn't quite define flashed in Lynette's eyes. "Because my nieces invited me." Her chin—

yes, *chin*, singular, she was still thin and striking even in her fifties—came up. "And it sounded like fun."

More wine slipped down Blythe's gullet. A soft, warm glow ensued. "*My* wedding was fun."

"Your wedding was a mistake," her mother said bluntly. Again, exactly like Nana. Forget falling far from the tree—this apple still had a death grip on the branch.

"You met Giles exactly once," Blythe said. Stubbornly. Stupidly. Considering the whole thing had been a mistake. And a colossal one at that.

"Which is all it took to know he was exactly like Ronald."

Irritation spiked…until Blythe realized her mother was right. Hell, Giles could have played her father in the movie, they were so much alike. Only at the time Blythe had been too besotted to see it. But the realization that her mother had, and still remained silent, galled her even more.

"So why didn't you say anything?"

"Would you have listened? Especially to me—?"

"You must be Blythe's mother," Wes said, appearing out of nowhere, hand extended, campaign grin on full display.

What the hell? At least her mother looked as nonplussed as Blythe felt.

"Yes, I am." Her reluctance obvious, she shook his hand. "Lynette Broussard. And you are…?"

"Wes Phillips." He slipped his hand into his pants' pocket. Still grinning. "Neighbor, five houses north. It's been great to watch the old inn come back to life. Your daughter's done a fantastic job with it. Not that I know a lot about design, but she certainly seems very talented to me. You should be very proud of her."

Her mother actually blushed. As well she should, since prior to the inn she'd never seen any of Blythe's work. Not her design work, anyway. And her attitude toward Blythe's earlier artistic endeavors had ranged from dismissive to uninterested. But now her eyes veered to Blythe's, followed by a small smile.

"Yes, she is. And I am."

Talk about your out-of-body experiences. And the wine wasn't helping—

"Good," Wes said, briefly touching Blythe's shoulder as he sauntered off, but not before giving her an I've-got-your-back look that seared her all the way through. Followed by a jolt to her midsection when she caught the all-too-knowing one in her mother's eyes. Lynette may have been aloof, but she wasn't an idiot.

"Now that one's *nothing* like your father," she said, watching Wes's departure for a moment before facing Blythe again. "We need to talk."

Blythe glowered at the shimmering liquid in her still half-full glass, then let out a sigh as she set it on a nearby table. Because running was running, no matter what form it took. She did, however, wobble back toward the wedding venue—not because she was tipsy, but because her heels kept gouging the damn grass—where she grabbed a folding chair out of Todd's hands before he could stack it on a cart, yanked it open and sank on it. Graciously, the bearded redhead opened another one for her mother, who'd followed.

Then Blythe leaned back in the chair, letting the breeze clear the muzzies from her brain, and waited for her mother to say whatever she had to say.

"Hate to tell you this, but your face might as well be a CNN news crawl right now."

Wes turned from watching Blythe and her mother to face the radiant, satin-gowned brunette at his side. The inn's long back porch, where they were doing cocktails and appetizers before dinner, gave him—and everyone else—an unobstructed view of the mother-daughter chat going on down on the lawn. But between the distance, the constant breeze and the thrum of conversation, listening in was not happening.

"Blythe ever talk about her relationship with her mother?"

"Not much," Mel said, leaning on the porch railing, cradling a glass of wine. "In fact, when we were kids she barely mentioned her childhood at all. I remember seeing Aunt Lynette once or twice, when she'd drop Blythe off at our grandmother's, but that was it. I don't think I ever actually spoke to her. Not a close family, as you may have gathered. Then the three of us lost touch for years, of course. And since we've reconnected…"

She took a sip of the wine. "Blythe's always given off this whole 'I'm so in control' vibe, but if you ask me there's a boatload of hurt simmering inside that woman."

"Simmering? Try a furious boil," Wes said.

Mel's brows rose. Wes wondered if her cousins knew about Blythe's "bad girl" years, decided this wasn't the time to bring them up. Nor was it his place to do so. Even so, Blythe's opening up to him had been gratifying, in a weird sort of way. If nothing else, she apparently trusted him. As much as he suspected she trusted anyone, that is.

As though reading his mind, Mel said, "As I said, she's never said much. But she's dropped enough hints to make April and me think she's had things a lot rougher than she lets on. That the people she should have been able to rely on let her down the most. I'm guessing nobody's ever, not once, put Blythe's needs ahead of their own."

"And I'd say your hunch is dead-on. And yet…she does for everyone else."

"Exactly." Her eyes slanted to his again. "I take it you do like her?"

Wes sighed. "You might say. Although she accused me of being fascinated by her. Intrigued."

"Are you?"

After a moment, Wes said, "Yes. In the same way complex math problems used to intrigue me as a kid. As though I can't rest until I figure her out."

That got a soft chuckle before Mel laid a hand on his wrist. "And right there is probably more than anyone else has ever given her. Let me tell you something about our Blythe—when we were kids, she used to lord it over us like nobody's business. Probably because, now that I think about it, that was one of the few ways she felt in charge of her own life. But she was also the big sister neither of us had. In a good way, I mean. She watched out for us and covered for us and would let us crawl in bed with her when it was storming or we'd had a nightmare. And it kills me to think she never had anyone do that for *her*."

"It does me, too," Wes said, watching as Blythe and her mother both stood, staring awkwardly at each other for a moment before Blythe stalked back toward the house, her gait hitching slightly when she realized he was watching her.

He sensed Mel's taking in the silent exchange before she said, "You could be the one to change all that for her, if you're so inclined. Because I can tell she's intrigued, too, by the possibility of finally getting what she's never had. Scared, but curious. But it won't be easy—"

"Wondered where you'd gotten off to," Ryder said, the dark-haired doctor coming up to slip an arm around his wife's waist. And, truth be told, envy pinched when Wes witnessed Mel's soft smile for her husband, even if the envy was almost immediately followed by another wave of determination.

"Considering my day job?" Wes said to Mel. "I wouldn't know 'easy' if it bit me in the butt."

Leaning into her husband's embrace, Blythe's cousin lifted her glass to him. "Then go get her, cowboy. And don't take 'no' for an answer."

But before he could do that—his gaze wandered out to the gazebo, where Blythe's mother stood by the railing, looking out over the water—there was someone else he needed to have a little chat with.

Lynette angled toward him as he approached, a suggestion of a smile on a face thinner than Blythe's, the bone structure more pronounced. "So my suspicions were correct," she said, facing the water again. "You're interested in my daughter."

Wes lowered himself to one of the built-in seats, tugging slightly at his tie in the rising temperature. "If I was only 'interested,' Ms. Broussard, I doubt I'd be here right now."

"With me, you mean?"

"Yes."

She smiled again, more fully this time, then sat as well, on the bench across from him. "She tells me you're in Congress."

"Three-quarters through my first term, yes."

"So you're up for reelection in November?"

"That's right."

Lynette's eyes narrowed, just slightly. "And you have a son?"

"Jack. He'll be twelve next month."

"That's quite a full plate, isn't it?"

Fighting a smile of his own, Wes nodded. If he wasn't mistaken, he was being interviewed. If not grilled. "If you're asking if there's room for your daughter on that plate, the answer is absolutely. And yes, I know all about her background."

"I see. And you don't think that could be an issue? For your career?"

The very question that had plagued him to the point of wondering how he'd been able to get any work done at all—let alone sleep—during the past week. But like those math problems that, as a kid, he'd refused to abandon unsolved, Wes refused to accept that there wasn't a solution to this one, as well. One that benefitted everyone.

"And what if I said that Blythe's worth that risk?"

Tears bloomed in Lynette's eyes before she stood again, leaning hard on the railing facing the water so Wes could only see her profile. He got to his feet, too, propping one shoulder on a support post with his arms crossed, his relaxed posture giving the lie to the anger seething inside.

"Blythe also told me why she did the things she did, in a desperate attempt to get her parents—you, in particular—to pay attention to her. To love her. That nothing worse happened—that nobody got hurt, that her spirit wasn't completely crushed—is a damn miracle."

Finally, Lynette looked at him, guilt screaming in her eyes. "I suppose you think she has every right to hate me."

Wes thought about that for a moment. "The right to? Maybe. Not my call. But do you think she does?" Slowly, Lynette shook her head. "I don't think so, either."

"And do you?" Lynette quietly asked.

"Hate you?"

"Yes."

"What I think," Wes said after a pause, "is that you and her father—and Blythe's actions, as a consequence—made an incredibly generous human being believe she's inherently unlovable. That she's not worth anybody's putting their butt on the line for her. And that breaks my heart. Not to mention makes me mad as hell."

Several seconds passed before Lynette sank back onto

the bench, hunched over her folded hands. "Believe it or not, it breaks my heart, too. That I couldn't see past my own pain to realize what I was doing to my daughter." She lifted her eyes to his. "I was a terrible mother, Wes. And I'm not sure I'll ever forgive myself for that. But if you can give her even some of what I never did, if you could… could…" Her eyes watered again. "If you could somehow help her find her way out of that dark place her father and I put her in, I'd be more grateful than I can say."

"There's nothing saying you can't still do that, you know."

Lynette gave him a weak smile. "In the time I have left? I doubt it."

Over the punch to his gut, Wes said, "Then I promise you, I'll do what I can," before he walked away.

Chapter Twelve

Two days later, Blythe slumped on Mel and Ryder's new couch, in their new house in town, trying to focus on some dance movie Quinn had picked from the On Demand cable menu. Except two days later she still hadn't been able to shake her unease over seeing Wes's making a beeline for her mother after the wedding. Or catching him talking to Mel before. Because no way could either of those things be good, or good for her.

Unfortunately, all she could do was sit here—in the same tank top and drawstring pajama bottoms she'd worn to bed—and speculate as Channing Tatum flexed his mighty fine muscles on Mel and Ryder's huge TV, since she doubted Mel would appreciate a "What the hell was all that about?" phone call on her honeymoon. Or any phone call, probably. And confronting her mother before she'd returned to Harper's Ferry had been an exercise in futility, since the woman had gone all cagey on her about what she and Wes had actually discussed.

Of course, she could call Wes himself, she supposed. Suuuuure she could. And say what, exactly? Act like some paranoid loser chick, demanding to be made privy to the conversations?

What was really pathetic, though, was how much it ticked her off that Wes hadn't contacted her himself. Especially since he knew *she* knew about both little conferences. And even if his chat with Mel hadn't involved Blythe, although she sincerely doubted that, she even more sincerely doubted that held true for the one with her mother.

And it was driving her crazy.

Craz*ier*.

Because she'd already made herself nuts missing him. Never mind that, even if she found the cojones to get over herself, her fears, everything else still held true. No matter what, her past would be a liability. And this guy...if she could believe what she'd read, what she'd heard, Wes was a true prince among men. Someone who'd make his son proud one day, if he hadn't already.

Someone who made her proud now—

"Blythe?" Quinn said, stuffing popcorn in her mouth. When Blythe scowled over at her, the girl jerked her head sideways. "The doorbell?"

Grabbing the bowl, Blythe crammed a handful in her own piehole. Or popcorn hole, in this case. "So answer it."

"And if I get killed," the girl said, unfolding herself from the couch to tromp across the room, "I'm telling Mom you made me."

Since the likelihood was higher that Channing Tatum would materialize in front of them, Blythe wasn't too worried. Until Quinn tramped back thirty seconds later and plopped back on the couch. "Jack's dad wants to talk to you."

Popcorn halfway to her mouth, Blythe froze. "What?"

The girl rolled her eyes. "Jack's dad. At the door. Asked if he could talk to you." Then she gave Blythe a quick scan. "Although you might want to fix yourself up first. You're kind of scuzzy. Ow!" she said when Blythe smacked her with a throw pillow, then climbed off the sofa, madly finger-combing her hair as she tramped to the vestibule, her heart stumbling to keep up. And God only knew what her brain was doing.

"I think 'scuzzy' might be overstating it," Wes said, grinning, when she got to the door. He was sexy as hell in a T-shirt and jeans, his hair all windblown, and everything... She shuddered. From love, from lust, from longing, the lot. "Although..." He did a quick body scan, then checked his watch. "It is three in the afternoon."

Belatedly remembering that she wasn't wearing a bra, Blythe crossed her arms over her chest. Stupid, she knew, since it wasn't as if he hadn't seen what lay beneath the thin jersey. "Hey. I brushed my teeth. Everything else is gravy. Especially since I'm not going anywhere. And why are you here?"

"For you."

"For...me."

"Sure as hell not for Quinn. No offense, honey," he shouted past Blythe's shoulder, and Quinn shouted back, "None taken."

"But..." Blythe was thoroughly confused. Turned on, but confused. "Nothing's changed."

"About how I feel about you? You got that right."

"Not what I meant."

Wes sighed. "You're going to make this difficult, aren't you?"

"Actually, I think you're the one making things difficult—"

She jumped a little when he slammed his hand onto the

doorframe, those lovely green eyes boring into hers. "Tell me you don't feel the same way about me and I'll walk away right now and never bother you again."

"For heaven's sake, Wes..." Blushing, Blythe angled her head toward Quinn.

"Good. She can be a witness. So? What's it going to be? The truth, Blythe. Not some save-your-butt BS."

"Wes!"

"It's okay," came from behind her. "I've heard worse, believe me—"

"And what if I do?" Blythe blurted out, her eyes stinging. "As I said, nothing's changed—"

"Then let's change it."

"How?"

Wes shrugged, accompanied by a grin that managed to be sheepish, adorable and dead sexy all at once. Could that mouth multitask or what? "Think I could persuade you to put on real clothes? So we could take a walk?"

"Can I come?" Quinn said.

"No," Wes said, then pinned Blythe again with that sweet, determined gaze. "Well?"

When her heart tried to leap in her chest, she smacked it back down. Because unless they'd both landed in some alternate universe over the past few days, she couldn't imagine what he wanted to say. However, Blythe could count on one hand those moments in her life she'd consider life-changing, even if the first few—when her father had walked out, when Travis Fallon had broadcast to everyone in school that she'd lost her virginity to him—had blind-sided her. Since then she'd gotten much better at reading the tea leaves, as it were, sensing the propitiousness before it actually hit. And if this wasn't one of those occasions, she'd eat that bra she wasn't currently wearing.

"All right," she said, then hustled back to the guest-room to throw on said bra, a sleeveless top, a long skirt and flip-flops. And, okay, some mascara. And a spritz of perfume. Thus upping the Seventh Layer of Hell vibe to maybe the Third.

"Do not answer the door while I'm gone," she called out as she smack-smacked past, grabbing her purse off the table by the front door. "And lock the door behind me."

"Oh, *now* you don't want me to answer the door," Quinn said, then grinned. "Have fun, you two."

"Brat," Blythe muttered as she followed Wes out onto the small front porch, choked with pots of bobbing petunias and pansies. The lock barely tumbled into place behind them before Wes took her face in his hands and kissed her. And there was promise in that kiss, by golly. A promise she'd sure as hell never felt from any other man before.

"Wes…what…?"

"Do you trust me?" he whispered.

"Yes," she said. Because God help her, she did.

He took her hand. "Then let's go."

And wherever he was taking her, she would follow.

She just hoped God was in an extra-special, helping kind of mood that day.

To some people, Wes supposed it would seem weird, if not disrespectful, to take Blythe back to the same beach where they'd run into each other before. Not because of how things had ended that day, but because it had meant so much to Wes and Kym. But the coincidence was too great to be ignored—that they had somehow run into each other on that beach. As though someone—Kym? God? Some unknown angel assigned to the case?—was saying, "You need to revisit this. Rethink it. Look at things in a new light."

So he had. Nonstop since his conversation with her mother. And the conclusion he'd come to was that if

Blythe's double rejection had forced him to dig deeper, to work harder for this woman who'd apparently never had anyone work very hard for her at all, then the temporary pain had been worth it.

Of course, nothing said she might not retreat a third time. There were no guarantees. But at least he'd know he'd tried, that he'd made his best offer. And she'd know he was serious.

That while she wasn't the only thing in his life that mattered, nothing mattered more.

"Your mother's quite a character," he said as they walked hand in hand along the water, their shoes dangling from their fingers.

"You brought me here to talk about my mother?"

"Don't see how we can move forward until we do." At Blythe's silence, Wes hazarded a glance. But she looked straight ahead, squinting slightly in the angled sun. "And I do want to move forward."

A funny smile played across her mouth. "As in, to pretend the past doesn't exist?"

"No, as in to say 'screw you' to it."

"Easier said than done," Blythe muttered, then said, "So what did she say? My mother?"

"How about you tell me what she said to you first?"

They came to a deserted dock; Blythe led Wes out onto it, then lowered herself onto the edge. Wes followed suit, waiting. "Did she tell you she'd been sick?" she said at last.

"Not directly, but I got the gist." He looked over. "You didn't know, did you?"

Looking toward the opposite shore, Blythe shook her head. "No. True, we didn't talk all that often, but that's kind of a major thing to keep your only child in the dark about."

"And she wouldn't be the first parent in the world to do that."

"I suppose. Except in this case it was one more example of how little our lives intersected. How little she wanted them to intersect. I mean, I would have been there for her, if she'd asked. Could have brought her up to D.C. to live with me, could have driven her to her radiation appointments..."

"You would have done that for her?"

"Of course. Why wouldn't I?"

He hesitated, then said, very carefully, "Still trying to win her love?"

"Still trying to be her daughter." Her mouth thinned. "That's all I ever wanted. Just some tiny—" she pinched her thumb and forefinger together "—acknowledgment of our relationship."

Wes took her hand, kissed it. "And maybe after everything that went down—or didn't—between you, she didn't think she had the right to ask that of you."

She met his gaze. "Is that what she said to you?"

"I'm pretty good at reading between the lines. She admitted she screwed up. And I gather she doesn't think time's on her side."

"For what?"

"To fix things between you."

At that, Blythe's hand went to her mouth, tears flooding her eyes. After a moment, she lowered it, whispering, "Then why didn't she say that to me?"

"Because she's scared?"

Blythe's waterlogged eyes remained steady on his. "She told me...she said she's okay now. But that's a lie, isn't it?"

"I don't know, honey. You could be right. But she did say..." He paused.

"Don't you dare stop there—"

"She said she hoped I could give you everything you never got from her or your father."

Blythe's first sob exploded from her throat like a rifle

shot, reverberating over the water as Wes hauled her close. How long had it been, he wondered, since she'd given all those bottled-up emotions their head? Long enough, apparently, that it took several minutes to cry herself out, the sobs finally giving way to a long, shuddering sigh as she laid her head on his shoulder. When he offered her his handkerchief, she gave a soggy laugh.

"Who the h-hell still carries cloth handkerchiefs?"

"I do. Shut up and blow. You're a mess."

Another shaky laugh preceded a lengthy blowing session, following by more sighing. "Why does love hurt so damn much?"

"It doesn't have to. In fact, rumor has it that sometimes it makes people very happy."

"Yeah, I've heard that rumor, too. Although I suppose…" She swallowed. "I suppose it helps if you know what you're looking for. Instead of, you know, settling for substitutes. Not sure which shrink pointed that out—probably all of them—but I finally realized that's what I was doing."

Gently rubbing her shoulder, Wes kissed the top of her head. "Are you worried that's what I am? Another substitute for the real thing?"

A long pause preceded, "No."

"So you love me?"

She winced. "You would ask me that."

"I sure as shootin' didn't ask you here to talk about the weather."

A short laugh preceded, "Yes. But—"

Wes brought her face around to look deep in her eyes. "Do you believe I love *you*?"

"How about…I want to? But—"

"If things were different, if I wasn't in politics, if you

weren't worried about your past…would you be willing to give 'us' a chance?"

Her pause felt interminable. Until, finally, she nodded. "Yes. Oh, yes. But—"

"Then enough with the 'buts.' Instead, options."

She reared back to frown at him through red, puffy eyes. "Options?"

Wes held up one finger. "Option one—I don't run for reelection."

"Wh-what?"

"You heard me. I give up my seat in the house and go back to my law practice right here in St. Mary's. Or Jack and I can relocate to D.C., whatever works best for you—"

"Are you *crazy?* No! Absolutely not! Of all the absurd…" She blew out a harsh breath, her forehead pinched. "I can't let you do that. These people, they need you. Need someone who really, truly has their best interests at heart. For you to walk away from them for me…" She crossed her arms. "No. No way. Not happening."

Wes smiled. "You sure?" When she glared at him, he chuckled. "All right. Then option number two—we turn the negative into a positive."

Her forehead crunched even more. "What does that mean?"

He pried her hand away from her stomach to entwine their fingers. "This is the hard one. For you, mostly. It means we come clean about your past before anyone has a chance to dig it up."

Blythe's eyebrows flew up. "You can't possibly be saying—"

"You want to help kids who feel disconnected? Then throw open that closet door, honey. Go public with your past. Show those kids how to turn their attitudes, their lives, around."

"You mean...sacrifice my privacy?"

"Initially, yes. That's why I said this would be harder on you. But I'm also talking about exploiting your greatest asset, which is your compassion. You remember when you told me about how, when you found that website, what it was like to realize you weren't alone? That there were other kids going through the same crap you were? Now imagine having an even bigger platform to help those kids you care about so much." He smiled, even as his heart was about to punch through his chest. "As my wife."

"As your *what?*"

"Wife. Okay, let's go with fiancée—it's too soon to plan a wedding before the election, anyway...where are you going?" he said when she jumped up and took off back down the pier, her skirt flying behind her.

"Away," she shouted over her shoulder. "Before I push you into the bay!"

Wes caught up before she reached land, spinning her around to see she was crying again. "Oh, hell, honey, it's okay...I didn't mean to push, but how else could I let you know how serious I was—?"

"You would risk your career for me?" She swiped at her eyes. "Or even *give it up?*"

"Yes to both."

"Why?"

"Because you're worth more than any of it. Because, after Kym, I never thought I'd find anyone with as much heart as she had. That may be the only thing the two of you had in common," he said on a soft laugh, "but it's also the only thing that matters. And I know what I'm asking of you, to lay your past on the altar. To lay yourself there, for that matter. That whole fishbowl thing—you're absolutely right about that. But I'll be right there with you. And *for* you. And frankly, if people can't deal with the woman

I love being a real human being with real issues—issues she overcame—then I don't want their votes."

She blinked. "You can't mean that."

"I've never meant anything more. Other than when I said I loved you. And I want you in my life. Mine and Jack's—"

"Oh, dear God—Jack!" Her eyes went wide. "Even if I agreed to your insane idea, how could I do that to a kid—?"

"How about giving the *kid* some credit? He already knows you were no Goody Two-shoes. If anything, my guess is that's what changed his mind about you. Because you're real. And honest. And living proof that people can triumph over their mistakes. Which we all make, honey. Because screwing up is what human beings do. And do not give me some malarkey about not thinking you'd be a good mother, because Jack and I can't think of anyone who'd make a better one." He crossed his arms. "So deal, sweetheart."

Then Wes rested, as he would have in any debate, thinking he'd never made a more importunate—or important—campaign speech in his life.

He could practically see the wheels turning in her brain. "I'm not giving up my career," she said, and Wes's breath rushed from his lungs. Then he chuckled.

"Unless you're secretly moonlighting as a stripper, I think we're good."

"With these boobs? As if."

Wes laughed again, then sobered. "Although this will be a challenge, honey, I'm not gonna lie. For all of us. And I can't guarantee how it will play out—"

"I know that," she said, then let out a long, slow breath. "Okay. Let's do this."

"This?"

"Or were you just yanking my chain about being your wife?"

Took him a second. "Are you sure?"

"Kiss me," she said. So he hauled her into his arms and did. Several times. "Mmm, yeah. I'm sure." She linked her hands around the back of his neck, smiling into his eyes. "Because like you said, screw the past."

"Amen to that," he said, grinning, and kissed her again.

Victory had truly never tasted so sweet.

Epilogue

"How is she?" Blythe asked breathlessly as she burst into the maternity wing's waiting room, eerily pearlized from the surprise snowfall the night before. Behind her, Wes and Jack followed.

Grinning, a five-months' pregnant Mel took her by the hand to lead her down the hall. "Mom and daughter are doing fine," she said, and Blythe got all misty-eyed. April had refused to find out whether she was having a boy or girl, which had made decorating the nursery somewhat challenging. Then again, she supposed the human race had muddled through for a long time—and nurseries had gotten decorated—without knowing what equipment their little bundles of joy would be coming with.

"Blythe! Ohmigosh, you're here!" From her hospital bed, a slightly rumpled April smiled, her arms filled with a tiny, pink-and-aqua-striped bundle. Patrick sat on April's right, so clearly entranced by his new daughter he barely glanced up at Blythe's entrance. And on her other side, an equally entranced kindergartner snuggled close to April's shoulder. "Come look!"

A tear slipped down Blythe's cheek as she eased herself onto the edge of the bed. Hormones, no doubt, she thought as April shifted the bundle into Blythe's arms, the baby giving an indignant little squeak. Then she opened her eyes and frowned, all dark and assessing, and Blythe laughed.

"Oh, April—she's gorgeous."

"Just like her mama," Patrick said, and April grinned even harder.

"Where are Wes and Jack?" she asked.

"Out in the hall, I didn't want to crowd you—"

"Don't be ridiculous, bring 'em in, for heaven's sake!"

Mel let them into the room as she let herself back out. But not before Blythe caught herself staring at her cousin's cute little baby bump. That one, they already knew was a girl. Meaning, so far two for three…

"Go on," April said, "let Wes hold her. After all, it's been twelve years since he's done this, he's probably gonna need a refresher course."

Blythe's gaze shot to her cousin's. She hadn't said a word to anyone yet. Not even Wes. But Wes was either ignoring her cousin's comment or it had gone right over his head as he cooed at the baby, gently bouncing her as he walked around the room.

Nope, no refresher course needed there.

"What's her name?" Jack asked, as fascinated with the baby as his dad.

April grinned. "Well, what with it being Valentine's Day and all—"

"You didn't," Blythe said, shooting a look at her cousin. "Valentine Shaughnessy?"

April and Patrick both laughed. "Oh, Lord, no. We're

naming her Rose. After Patrick's grandmother on his daddy's side."

Blythe sat on the arm of Wes's chair, letting the infant grab hold of her finger. "Welcome to the world, little Rose."

Then Wes looked up at Blythe and winked, and she flushed.

She'd been dead serious, all those months ago, when she'd told Wes she couldn't see herself as a mother. Nor, despite how easily she'd assumed the role of Jack's mom, had Wes exerted even the slightest pressure for more babies. Even though Blythe knew, because his mother had let it slip one day, that he and Kym had wanted more children. Except Jack's birth had been so difficult they'd decided not to try again. But not long after Wes's and Blythe's low-key wedding in November—in front of the same justice of the peace who'd married her cousins—it finally dawned on her how often humans trick themselves into believing they don't want what they think they can't have.

And how had she missed that the whole point of rebellion was to break free? Not to become fear's prisoner.

At the baby's feed-me squawk, Patrick carefully lifted her out of Wes's arms and handed her back to April, who put the infant to her breast as though she'd been doing it her entire life. She'd finally come clean to her cousins about her past, which naturally resulted in some verbal smackdowns about not trusting them, jeez. Another lesson learned about what it means to be a real family, she supposed, her eyes burning with love for all these people she'd finally found the courage to let completely into her heart. Her soul.

"We'll see you later," Blythe said as she squeezed her cousin's hand, her insides squeezing as well at the sight.

That, by Halloween, if not sooner, would be her.

A thought that brought wonder, panic, joy...and a little

sorrow, that her own mother would never meet her grand-child.

Although a few weeks couldn't make up for nearly thirty years, if the long—and long overdue—talks Blythe and her mother shared before her passing in September brought Lynette some peace, Blythe was glad. Whether her mother ever truly loved her, even at the end, she didn't know. But if Lynette had finally accepted *Blythe's* love, perhaps that was the grace she needed to find.

Just as it apparently had been Blythe's, she thought as they left the hospital, Wes taking her hand as they crossed the parking lot. Jack saw it, rolling his eyes even as he grinned. Smiling herself, Blythe gave her stepson a quick, one-armed hug, letting go before he blushed.

So far, the kid had been a total champ about everything—Blythe's past, the preemptive strike "plan" that had worked even better than they'd hoped during the election campaign, his finally coming to terms with his father's career. Although Wes and Blythe had considered making Washington their full-time home, putting Jack in school there, Jack had insisted he was fine with things the way they were. He wanted to stay in St. Mary's with his grandparents, so he could go to the same school, hang with his friends—at least, those whose parents *weren't* douche bags. Including, but no longer limited to, Quinn, which frankly made everyone breathe easier.

For now, anyway.

They dropped Jack with his grandparents before continuing on to the little bed-and-breakfast in Annapolis where they'd spent their weekend honeymoon right after the election. A Valentine's Day treat, Wes had told her that morning, surprising her. A night to themselves, a tiny oasis of time in the midst of the chaos that was their lives.

And it was only going to get more chaotic, Blythe

thought as Wes held out her chair for her in the eighteenth-century tavern-turned-restaurant a block from the B&B.

She'd awakened that morning to find him at the foot of her bed. Grinning. And naked, a gorgeous bouquet of roses covering his fun bits. This was a man who knew how to do Valentine's Day.

And now it was her turn.

"I'm sorry, I only got a card," she said, handing it to him across the table, taking care to avoid the votive candle in the middle.

"It's okay," he said with a wink, "I got my present this morning...what's this?" Giving her a funny look, he opened the bulky envelope, then the card.

Wrapped in a double-seal baggie, her positive pregnancy test clunked onto the table in front of him.

Blythe bit her lip, trying not to laugh at his flummoxed expression before his eyes shot to hers.

"You're kidding?"

"It's sure as heck not somebody else's pregnancy test."

"But I thought...you were on the Pill?"

"I stopped it. Two months ago."

His eyes softened. "You meant to get pregnant?"

"I did," she said, smiling, as happiness the likes of which she'd never known bubbled up inside her. At the love in Wes's eyes, the promise in her belly. A girl, she hoped. The next generation of "sisters," who'd share sunblock and secrets, heartaches and triumphs. And love.

So much love.

Wes reached for Blythe's hand across the small table, pressing his mouth to her knuckles. "Do you have any idea how much I love you?"

Tears burning her eyes, she touched his face. "Yes," she whispered, smiling. Accepting.

The waitress brought their dinners, congratulating them

when Wes, so excited Blythe thought her heart would burst, told her their news…and everyone in the tiny restaurant applauded. If Blythe's hunch was correct, she and Wes and whatever kids came along would never have a "regular" life. And that was just fine with her.

Because this life promised to be better than anything she could have ever imagined.

* * * * *

REQUEST YOUR FREE BOOKS!

2 FREE NOVELS PLUS 2 FREE GIFTS!

◊ HARLEQUIN®

SPECIAL EDITION

Life, Love & Family

In Buckshot Hills, Texas, a sexy doctor meets his match in the least likely woman—a beautiful cowgirl looking to reinvent herself....

Enjoy a sneak peek from USA TODAY *bestselling author Judy Duarte's new Harlequin® Special Edition® story,* TAMMY AND THE DOCTOR *, the first book in* Byrds of a Feather, *a brand-new miniseries launching in March 2013!*

***

Before she could comment or press Tex for more details, a couple of light knocks sounded at the door.

Her grandfather shifted in his bed, then grimaced. "Who is it?"

"Mike Sanchez."

Doc? Tammy's heart dropped to the pit of her stomach with a thud, then thumped and pumped its way back up where it belonged.

"Come on in," Tex said.

Thank goodness her grandfather had issued the invitation, because she couldn't have squawked out a single word.

As Doc entered the room, looking even more handsome than he had yesterday, Tammy struggled to remain cool and calm.

And it wasn't just her heartbeat going wacky. Her feminine hormones had begun to pump in a way they'd never pumped before.

"Good morning," Doc said, his gaze landing first on Tex, then on Tammy.

As he approached the bed, he continued to look at Tammy,

his head cocked slightly.

"What's the matter?" she asked.

"I'm sorry. It's just that your eyes are an interesting shade of blue. I'm sure you hear that all the time."

"Not really." And not from anyone who'd ever mattered. In truth, they were a fairly common color—like the sky or bluebonnets or whatever. "I've always thought of them as run-of-the-mill blue."

"There's nothing ordinary about it. In fact, it's a pretty shade."

The compliment set her heart on end. But before she could think of just the perfect response, he said, "If you don't mind stepping out of the room, I'd like to examine your grandfather."

Of course she minded leaving. She wanted to stay in the same room with Doc for the rest of her natural-born days. But she understood her grandfather's need for privacy.

"Of course." Apparently it was going to take more than simply batting her eyes to woo him, but there was no way Tammy would be able to pull off a makeover by herself. Maybe she could ask her beautiful cousins for help?

She had no idea what to say the next time she ran into them. But somehow, by hook or by crook, she'd have to think of something.

Because she was going to risk untold humiliation and embarrassment by begging them to turn a cowgirl into a lady!

***

Look for TAMMY AND THE DOCTOR from
Harlequin® Special Edition® available March 2013

♦ HARLEQUIN®

SPECIAL EDITION

Life, Love and Family

Look for the next book in
The Fortunes of Texas: Southern Invasion miniseries!

After a broken marriage, Asher Fortune moves to
Red Rock, where he needs someone to help him
and his four-year-old son, Jace, start a new life.
He knew upon their first meeting that Marnie was
great for Jace, but he didn't realize what was in
store for *him!*

A Small Fortune
by *USA TODAY* bestselling author
Marie Ferrarella

*Available March 2013 from Harlequin Special Edition
wherever books are sold.*

HSE657285